HIS SLOTH

DEMON'S SIN BOOK 2

I0554285

AVA HUSH

This is a work of fiction. Any references made to real people, places, things, events, conversations are a fictitious byproduct of the author's imagination.

Cover by GetCovers
Editing & Proofreading by Courtney Humphreys
Beta Reading by Sarah Hansohn-White

AvaHushBooks.com

CONTENTS

CONTENT WARNINGS

- Mention of death of parent - violent, historic
- Rough sexual play and some sexual experimentation, all consensual.
- BDSM components/ references
- Descriptions of torture and abuse
- Abstract religious ideologies

This book is intended for Adult (18+) readers.

CHARACTERS

Aridam - wrath demon, mate of Rhys
Rhys - partial null, mate of Aridam
Azvameth - sloth demon, mate of Zhen
Zhenechka (Ivan) - soul mage / vampire hybrid, mate of Azvameth
Devland - greed demon
Kek – pride demon
Drystan - gluttony demon
Kieran - lust demon
Belial - envy demon

Astaroth - duke of Hell
Lily - witch, friend of alpha team
Franco - pride demon, Astaroth's assistant
Taylor - fae, friend of Rhys, damaged soul
Beckett - timber wolf shifter, damaged soul
Silas - arctic wolf shifter, damaged soul
Dane - timber wolf shifter, damaged soul
Joseph – scottish wolf shifter, damaged soul
Shax - envy demon, beta team
Helel - pride demon, beta team
Allocer - Duke of Hell, in charge of shadowlings
Mammon - Duke of Hell, in charge of new souls & demon children

Zadkiel - Angel of Righteousness
Raphael - Angel of Healing
Michael - Angel of Death
Gabriel - First Commander of the Angels
Azrael - Second Commander of the Angels
Chamuel - Third Commander of the Angels

Constantine D'arius - vampire coven leader, evil mastermind, dead
Alpha Gregory - Alpha of the Albany pack, sold his pack members to Constantine

Felicity Bianchi - witch, Italy's coven leader

ACKNOWLEDGEMENTS

To my editor, Courtney, for going above and beyond and helping a new author achieve her dreams.

SYNOPSIS

Azvameth

Constantine's operation was so much bigger than we could have imagined. Trying to untangle the web of evil around this mess is hard enough; add in the most disastrous first meeting of a fated mate in the history of fucking ever and now I FEEL shit? Hard pass. I'd rather go back to normal but reality doesn't seem to be so inclined. Wish me luck.

Zhenechka

Finally being free was supposed to make my life better. I no longer have an insane vampire controlling my every move, so why do I feel so lost? The only thing I can do is help the poor souls I've destroyed over the years, continue my research, and just hope I can eventually earn the mate I thought I'd lost my chance at having.

Chapter One

Azvameth

I'm bored. It's not a new sensation; I'm quite literally always fucking bored . . . Well, I guess unless I'm killing something. I flick through the channels on the hotel's TV, not settling on anything in particular. I keep this hotel room specifically for hookups and getting away from everyday annoyances. People are just so people-y it's disgusting. Interacting with others is not my strong suit unless it's during sex, and sometimes not then either.

Last night's interaction is still bothering me, unfortunately. The pretty brunette demon and her overly muscled shifter partner are tangled up in each other on the bed, sleeping. Their soft snores grate on my nerves. I could just kill them, but that's a lot of cleanup.

Threesomes aren't anything new for me. Group sex is more interesting in theory than it is in practice, though. I mean, maybe the first few times it was fun, but after almost four hundred years, it's just a lot of work with little to no gain. At least the demon was down for trying some "kinky shit." If you can call hair pulling and spanking kinky anymore. The shifter spent most of the night trying to top me, which I would normally be down for, but he was angling for domination like he wanted to put me in my place. No wonder she was looking for a third, if his prowess last night is anything to go by.

I sigh, bringing my attention back to the TV and clicking it off. I'll just head to the team house or to the witch's place. Maybe I'll get to bloody something or someone today. There's probably a meeting I'm missing, though, if the vibrations coming from the coffee table are any indication. Eh, I don't want to just sit around a table and talk. Gross. I lean over to deny Belial's millionth call. I need a shower and maybe something to eat before dealing with the team's bullshit.

The bathroom is almost blinding with the white-on-white color palate all hotels seem to insist on. At least there's a towel warmer. I flick the water on to let it warm up, the water pressure hard enough to be enjoyable. Honestly it's one of the biggest perks of keeping the room. Water pressure in Hell sucks.

Once the temperature is just the way I like it, I slide under the spray, taking my time. Hotel toiletries are abysmal, but I'll use them. Soaping up my body, I let my mind wander. My team lead, Aridam, has recently found his mate. If you had asked me before if anyone could tame the infamous wrath demon, I would have laughed in your face. Now, though? The little Null has most of the team wrapped around his finger. The first time I met him, he actually bossed Wrath around when he was riding the line between controllable and feral. Pity he succeeded; it's always entertaining watching the team try to calm Wrath down. Now my fun has been curbed by the human. A word from him and Wrath turns into a purring kitten. I would never make the mistake of thinking he's turned soft—it would be a fatal error. His intelligent grey eyes are just as ruthless as always, unless they're pointed at his mate. I can't imagine changing so much for another person. I've never met another sloth demon with a mate, though, so the point is probably moot anyway.

Deciding to skip washing my hair, I flick the water off. I dry myself quickly, throwing the towel on the floor of the bathroom atop the growing pile so housekeeping doesn't have to track them all over the place once I finally let them in. I wander back out to the living area, not bothering to dress, and pause in the doorway to the bedroom.

The two supes are going at it again, the wolf pounding into his greed demon with force. The lean lines of his body should excite me; her bouncing tits should beckon me to join. Too bad my dick isn't interested, not giving even a twitch. I'm not surprised. Honestly I could take or leave sex in general at this point. The dance of "will they, won't they" is so irritating. I hate games. The direct approach is my preference, but very few share my views. *I like your ass, let's fuck. Can I tie you to the wall and make you choke on my dick? I enjoy tears from time to time.* It's all frowned upon, unfortunately.

Sloth demons have a reputation for extreme kink or thrill-seeking play, and I used to fit that bill, but even the most extreme things lost my interest after a few years.

The couple is now moaning loudly and putting on a show. Wolf man is staring me down, likely believing he's responsible for her porn-star act and wanting to make me jealous. I scoff. Meh, I'm out. I don't bother with niceties or goodbyes, just quickly grab my phone and portal home to grab clothes. I know they'll leave the place intact, greed demon or not. They won't risk pissing me off.

Once dressed in whatever I could grab first, I head out. I don't bother checking my outfit in the mirror, as I only own neutral colors, so I know it matches. If it doesn't "go," then I don't care. Kek can suck it.

Entering the meeting room at the witch's shop, I notice Kek and Rhys are missing. I would feel bad about hurting Rhys's feelings yesterday by being abrupt, but it would be a waste of time. He'll get over it. I settle in one of the remaining seats, growing impatient at the lack of meeting actually taking place. I'm assuming it's about the run we went on at the deserted Colorado coven's compound, so I'd rather get this done so we can actually go after Constantine. My fingers itch to do something. After the remaining two join us, we finally get to the plan-making part. It takes a hot second, and I'm distracted repeatedly by the sense of calm Rhys projects. His effect on Belial is almost startling.

Envy isn't strangling me, so my jealousy toward the couple across the table is purely my own. Their mate bond is beautiful to see, but I slap myself mentally. It won't do any good to dwell on what I can't have. I clap my hands, getting myself and everyone else back on track. "So we scout ahead, Belial does his tech nerd magic, and we hit two places at once as a distraction. It leaves the third team to slip in and grab the souls. We have no idea what condition we will find them in. Team one is myself and Drystan; team two is Kieran and Aridam."

Nods and accenting murmurs meet my summary. Good. Rhys seems to be talking to himself, but his words get louder as he goes on. "Maybe 'sneaky smother fucker' is a skill they'll appreciate." I snicker and Kieran nudges him out of his trance. The whole discussion relaunches because the little human wants to be included. I stay out of it. It doesn't matter to me as long as he's not placed on my team.

After a lot of back and forth, it's decided that the little Null will be accompanying Kek and Devland to extract the souls.

We severely underestimated how many vampires were here. We knew some would be juiced up on supe blood, but the sheer number is staggering. After fighting for a while, I'm starting to wane. A pair of vampires rush me, veering apart at the last second, causing me to split my focus. No matter. The poor, poor, stupid vampire in front of me is split clean in half.

My claws are significantly sharper than other demons'; like paring knives, they slice through flesh like butter. While I'm taking apart the blonde vamp in front of me, the red-haired one behind me gets a good slice in. The blade is obsidian; the burning feeling left behind is unmistakable.

Six more vampires break off from the group headed for Aridam and blur to me. This fight stopped being great fun about ten seconds ago. Fuck.

"Drystan! A little help here!" His demon form is huge, rivaling the wrath demon in size. I know he still has his gluttonous urges restrained, though, because his movements aren't as ravenous or fluid as they should be. He's going to get us killed.

I continue to slice everything in front of me, using my wings as a shield over my shoulders. My back is only partially protected, and my wings are taking quite a few hits.

"Drys, come on!" I hate asking for help, but I'm not too proud to ask when my life is on the line.

A bone-chilling shriek sends relief coursing through my veins. Ahh, there he is. The vampires attacking me shift for a second to assess the new threat, giving me an opening to slaughter them all. I take care of my six with a smile, then step back and let Drystan do his thing. No way am I getting between a gluttony demon and his prey. I'll step in if he needs it, but I'd just piss him off if I didn't let him get his fill.

I hobble over to lean against the brick exterior of the giant house. My comm crackles as Belial issues updates to the whole team. My comm is usually quiet because he knows I'll rebel against any direct orders just on principle, so when it goes off, I do try to pay attention. Apparently Devland and Rhys found the cells, so I tune out anything else. I take a survey of the remaining vamps and realize some are fleeing. Stupid bloodsuckers.

Feeling more rested and a little gleeful, I sprint around to pick them off. I herd a few of the others back to Drys to take care of because I'm just that nice. The best, really. He shows no appreciation for my sacrifice, just hums and continues doing his thing. Ungrateful ass. Once they're in pieces, the gluttony demon seems to slow, a satisfied gleam in his smile.

My comm crackles in my ear once again. "Get to Rhys! Fuck! Damnit, he's not alone! DEVLAND, GET TO RHYS!" Belial's panicked tone in my earpiece turns into a rage-filled roar by the end. Shit. Sharing a quick look with Drys, I sprint to the house.

"Bel, where are they?" I don't actually dislike the human, and I can't stand the thought of one of my team seriously being hurt, so I'm putting all the pep into my step.

"Downstairs. He's not in camera view. When you get to the bottom, turn right. He said there was another bookshelf . . . hurry, Az." I'm already running down the stairs, taking three at a time. A dangerous roar sounds outside from Wrath. Shit, shit, shit. My heart is beating way too fast as I survey the room. A small body lies on the ground near the center of the room, and a group of people are huddled in the corner. A large wolf guards the group.

"Where is he?" I demand of him.

"We didn't see anything, just a blur and a hooded dark figure hitting him and taking off again. There was nothing we could do."

Kek and Devland rush into the room, wildly looking around. The roaring outside hasn't subsided. In fact, it's gotten so strong that the whole place is shaking. I need to help get everyone out before the house comes down, so I direct my attention to Kek.

"Rhys is gone. Now, I assume these are your missing souls." I gesture to the group, then turn to pick up the unconscious fae still lying on the floor. I hand him off to the pride demon, giving him a disgusted look as I do. I can't hold it back. He only had two jobs and managed to fuck up both. "Go before Wrath finds you." Devland pales at my words, quickly grabbing the hand of a random shifter from behind the big wolf and portaling out. I try to reassure the remaining supes, knowing that's what the others would do, but I'm not that great at pep talks. "He's taking them to safety. Our duke will be there to help sort this shit out shortly . . . hopefully. Go with them." I look at the lead wolf, knowing it'll be up to him to figure out who goes when and to calm the rest since my vague assurances didn't seem to help.

"I'll go last." How noble. I shrug. Doesn't matter to me.

I head back to the main level, checking bedrooms for any missed vamps. Wrath will kill everyone outside, friend or foe, so I'll be avoiding going out there right now, thank you. The deafening sound of a demon separated from his mate shakes the walls yet again. The gaudy gold chandelier in the entry sways violently as I skirt past the foyer. A huge crash draws my attention, as it sounds like it's coming from inside the house this time. I pick my way over to where I heard the ruckus, carefully avoiding the possible trajectories of the chandelier in case it does come down.

In the kitchen I find the source of the loud noise. Wrath has thrown a fucking tree through the brick mansion. Dammit. I back away, listening intently for his movements. I don't want to abandon him quite yet, but his tantrum could kill me if I'm not careful. I find a large bay window in the sitting room that gives a perfect view of Wrath's rampage without letting him see me. Drystan is also watching. I spot him hovering across the courtyard. I can't see Kieran. A sliver of worry wiggles through me.

"Bel, status on Kieran," I request softly, looking around the sitting room. Opulence that will be leveled by the day's end.

"Here with me. He's injured."

Phew. "All right. I'm going to head to the team house and reach out to our other contacts in the area. Hopefully they've spotted Rhys or Constantine."

"Noted. How is he?" There's no need to ask who. I double-check the courtyard and watch Wrath throw statues at the remaining vampires like bowling balls at unfortunate pins. He's also racing around, decapitating every single one after they fall.

"Umm . . . busy. Drystan is here; he's got him."

"Got it. Keep me posted."

I open a portal and slip through to the sound of Wrath's roar and the sweet screams of dying vampires.

Zhen

"Ivan, bind his wrists and place him on the hooks."

I hate him. I cannot help but comply with Constantine's demand, as he leaves no wiggle room. I try to only bind his wrists as tightly as is necessary to keep him hanging, carefully wrapping twice. I've noticed it doesn't cut off as much circulation as only wrapping once. As satisfied as I will get, I lift the poor

15

human by the forearms and settle the rope over the rusted meat hooks I assume were installed for skinning game. Hopefully the little tweaks make it more comfortable for him, but I cannot risk double-checking or going any slower than I am. Constantine has been watching my every move, and I'm lucky he hasn't called me out for being kinder than necessary. He has before. I've only been made to torture myself in this particular room once for trying to "skirt his commands," but that was years ago and thankfully it didn't last very long.

"What do you make of him? Give me your opinion." The coven leader's voice is oily and a little smug.

I grit my teeth, trying to withhold my response. It's no use. "He's bonded. The mating mark on his neck is quite fresh, less than a month. His blood smells pure, like clean copper. He's a human, but more. I have a theory but do not feel comfortable sharing until I gather more evidence. Scent alone is not sufficient."

"Speak plainly, hybrid. I dislike your science speak immensely."

"He's bonded to one of the demons. Meaning he won't die as fast . . . He might be more than human, but he smells purely human. The only thing I can think of is a Null."

"A Null, you say? How perfect. Let him wake organically. I wish to watch him when he feels he's alone. I wonder which idiot demon led their mate into a trap like that." He cackles like the green witch I saw in a movie once.

I cannot respond because he did not request for me to. I can only stand there, still, while I wait for my next order. He circles the human, leering at his body. "Remove all his clothing and begin to gather blood. You'll test your theory about him being a Null after we collect enough. I want it regardless. Either it gives us a boost or we die. You'll be our test subject."

I blink. At least I'm awaiting death with open arms. It would be a kind end, to die by consuming blood. It would be quick . . . much quicker than however Constantine plans to dispose of me eventually.

He leaves me to my task, knowing I cannot disobey him. After the human is bare, I begin to make small cuts along the parts of his legs that will give the correct amount of blood with the least pain. I avoid all joints and major arteries. I pull the only clean bucket from against the wall and place it under his hanging legs. I can't help but notice his soft skin, unblemished before today. My heart aches for him.

After I'm done, I wait. My next order will no doubt be cruel, for both the poor human and me. I can barely remember what it feels like to be free. It's been twenty years since I was taken and turned. Although I'm able to continue some of my research into supernatural genetics—encouraged, even—I've lost the passion for it. Science has always been my first love. I left my family coven to attend a university at the ripe age of fifteen and never looked back. I devoured knowledge like a starving man, trying to find the answers to the paranormal universe . . . starting with why our family line was different.

I knew we didn't practice magic the same as other witches, and looking back, I think my mother knew.

She knew what we were and chose to keep it to herself, not share it with future generations. Very cloak and dagger. I'll never get answers as to why, and it guts me. As always, when I think of my family, I'm bombarded with memories of the worst day of my life since it was the last day of theirs.

While my parents and siblings are still inside, I step into the sunroom of the family home to take a call from a colleague at the lab. I'm waiting for Petr to give me the results of the last tests, when a shadow moves outside, catching my eye. I squint and use the power that comes easiest to me to part the falling snow like a curtain. Several forms wait right behind our tree line. The hairs on the back of my neck stand up, and I end the call with Petr without a word. I need to concentrate.

I continue the farce of being on the phone, sending a draft of wind into the house as quietly as I can. I need one of them to notice. Nothing. Still no movement from the dark figures. What are they waiting for? Refusing to look away from the group out of the corner of my eye and lose the advantage, I try another draft, this time as cold as I can manage, hoping to garner anyone's attention, but my highest hope is my brother's. Silence reigns inside. I let out a relieved breath.

Slow, measured footsteps approach the hall. By the lack of weight to them, I suspect it is my sister Marina. I've never known for sure because when the footsteps finally reach halfway down the hall, the figures burst into action.

"Go! Bezhat!" I shout, not needing the silence anymore. Whoever is there listens, sprinting away.

The figures finally come into focus as they speed toward the house. Vampires. I gather the blowing snow with my magic and focus it at them, creating a blizzard in our backyard. My efforts seem to be slowing them down, but they show no sign of stopping. I imagine arrows and watch as they form in the ice drawn from the air. I start shooting them as fast as I can manage while still hitting my targets.

A scream sounds inside, followed by a crash. I drop my focus for a short moment, terrified that my family has been taken over from the front. I gather more strength and cause the earth beneath some of our attacker's feet to move at my whim. They manage to correct themselves, drawing nearer at an alarming pace, and I shout in frustration.

A lone vampire finally reaches the door and pulls it off its hinges. I don't wait before attacking, blasting him with what I can from inside, but he's too fast, dodging my elements with ease.

My chest caves with his first blow, launching me a few feet before I slam into the giant picture windows. Trying to catch my breath, I'm unable to prepare for the vicious attack that follows. His mouth hits my neck at the same time his hand enters my chest from the front. A scream rips from me unbidden. His hand moves to play with my organs as he gathers mouthfuls of blood from my neck. I can't move, and panic fills me.

His attention is suddenly diverted, and I'm tossed to the side, unable to do anything but stare out the windows at the falling flakes that float peacefully once again outside.

The continued screams inside are chilling as they abruptly cut off one by one. My brother Vladik was gifted with death magic like a necromancer. I was holding out hope that out of all of us, he would have the best defense against the vampires, but it proved to be just a myth, obviously.

I struggle to keep my eyes open. I stay conscious as long as I can, but eventually I succumb to my injuries and pass out.

I'm pulled out of my reverie by Constantine's voice as he re-enters the room. "He'll wake soon, Ivan."

Ivan. Not remotely my real name, but one I've been called for two decades. I repeat my given name and some basic information in my head as to not forget who I really am. Zhenechka Morozov. Forty-three years old—twenty as a vampire hybrid. Son of the head of the Morozov Coven.

I watch the human's breathing change, hear his heartbeat skip and his blood pressure increase. He's faking sleep, which would be smart if he wasn't in the company of vampires. I truly hope he makes it through this. I adjust my vision slightly to look at his soul. It's bright, pure, beautiful. His soul bonds are strong. One silver, one gold.

I have never divulged my ability to see and touch souls to anyone other than my mother. I followed her advice and told no one else. I always worked in secret and never spoke of it again . . . not even to her. I don't know the extent of this ability, just what I've been able to learn in the wee hours while everyone else is sleeping. Reading souls has become second nature and has helped me keep Constantine's test subjects alive in the past. It's not enough anymore to simply keep them alive. With this one, I'll do everything I can to help him make it out of here. He doesn't deserve any of this. No one does . . . and it's just the beginning.

Chapter Two

Azvameth

"Fuck! I think they found something!" Kieran takes off outside, no doubt running to aid the others since the shout we heard was a mix of victory and panic. We're finally at the farmhouse where Rhys is being held. Got a fancy angel escort to it and everything. We know he's here on the grounds, but we don't know who or what else is. All the running around aimlessly is a waste of time, so I don't follow Kieran out.

I have two more rooms to search, and I won't miss anything because I was rushing. I run my claws soundlessly against every surface in this tragically decorated bedroom. Like an explosion of pink flowers you'd find in every grandma's house on TV. Even I know it's awful. I retreat from the room only when I'm certain there's nothing hidden. Constantine has proven to be attached to hidden rooms and passages, so I will check every crease of wallpaper and every bookcase until I find it. Every house of his we've searched has had some sort of hidden *something*. This can't be the only one without.

Almost tripping over the gaudy floor runner, I glare at it as I slip into the blue version of the last room. Yuck. Even the bed skirt is blue floral. I make my way around, and everything moves freely against the walls, nothing mounted. I sigh, checking under the bed. Nope. What if? I lift the old-school rug and let it flop back, disappointed to see nothing once again. I had to have missed something. I retrace my steps in my head and realize I never checked under the detestable pink rug. Sigh.

 I deliberate the merits of checking again, but I give in and turn to head back, and something catches my eye. Symbols on the back of the door. Huh. I trace the marks with the pads of my thick fingers. They look like they were carved with a knife. Not exactly precise but close enough. The marks almost look like lettering. I pull out my phone to snap a picture. Maybe Belial will know. I'll quickly check that pink rug, then head out front to help the others if I don't find anything.

I hurry back to the pink room, lifting the rug and almost dropping it again before noticing something off. The floorboards are a little skewed, like a few planks have been replaced. I slide a claw between the boards. No illusion and it's flimsy, but I guess hidden under a bed and an old lady rug seemed good enough. I brace myself to be hit with a magical attack as I lift open the trap door, but it seems I've been spared. I switch seamlessly into my smaller human form, needing to be able to fit into the narrow space. Sounds filter up as I wiggle under the bed, which I had to wedge up with a close-by musty trunk, making as little noise as possible.

"What do you want?" Our wrath demon's growl gets louder as I slide down the incredibly narrow wooden stairs. I use every bit of my training and focus to make myself as invisible as possible. Being a sloth demon has a few perks besides the claws and extra enhanced hearing. I give off an irritated "go away, look away" kind of energy, making people naturally not focus on me at all if I leak it out in small, controlled doses. I just have to be careful how much I let out; otherwise it blows up in my face and has the opposite effect.

"Simple. I want what every vampire wants. Power and blood. I was well on my way to finding the best blood sources. Alas, I didn't have demon samples to compare. All I need is a few vials of your blood, plus a vial from each of your friends. See? Not too hard. You won't even feel it." I roll my eyes. He won't live long enough for any of this.

"That's it? You'll give me Rhys once you get the vials?" I continue to monitor my breathing as Aridam speaks, never altering my pattern, matching Constantine himself. Matching breathing patterns makes people believe theirs is the only one happening.

I focus on the vampire helping the coven leader and almost gasp and fuck this all up. Awareness travels through me. *Mine.* No! This vile vampire is my mate?! What the fuck? My mind spins. What was his name? Did anyone say?

"No, I'll be keeping this little morsel for a while longer. He's simply delicious. I could keep him in this state for years, at the cusp of survival. It's touch and go right now, but if he survives the day, he'll survive being my personal blood pet. I'll treat him with as much kindness as he does me. Who knows? Maybe he'll grow to like it since I can't compel him to. Makes no difference to me." Constantine sneers.

The giant vamp's arm twitches. It draws my reluctant attention. I try to focus on the words coming from my friend, but I'm not doing the best job, admittedly. My mate's smell is throwing me off balance. He smells of vampire and . . . something else? It's not bad necessarily, just confusing.

"Compulsion. That's something you do well, right? I mean, you'd have to, to control a vampire past their volatile transformation years. Ivan is what, twenty? That's a gift a demon might have, not a vampire. Yet here we are. So I wonder . . . would your compulsion die with you?" Aridam says.

What is Aridam going on about? What he's spouting is impossible. It doesn't change much for me, knowing compulsion on other vamps works for a couple hours at best. Regardless, Constantine dies now that I have an opening. I silently take the remaining two steps forward, swinging my right hand up and to the left with all my might, switching to my demon form as I do so.

"Ivan is a special breed—" My claws slice through his neck and up the left side of his jaw, removing his head right off his shoulders. My claws drip with blood and brain matter, and chunks of his skull are stuck to the tips of my middle two fingers. I flick them to the right, away from my mate . . . Ivan. Constantine said Ivan.

Ari makes a clicking noise, cluing me in to his displeasure of not killing the coven leader himself. I watch him and follow his murderous gaze to my mate. Fuck! Rhys's neck is bleeding, and the vamp is still holding the knife. Ivan's face blanches, and he tosses the weapon away, jumping back. I rush to place myself between the enraged wrath demon and my mate, steering the vamp a few feet away. His pale-green eyes remind me of sea foam. I get lost in them for a second before shaking my head.

"Are you hurt?" I'm disgusted that this vampire is what fate decided I was stuck with forever, but I'm more annoyed with myself for caring about him for even a second. Doing the bidding of another vampire is impossible after like two years. Compulsion doesn't work like that against another vampire, so he has to be incredibly weak-willed. Yet part of me aches for him. Even though we're the same size in my human form, he seems so fragile in this moment. He starts shaking and tears fill his eyes.

"I'm so sorry, *izvinite*. *Plez*. Don't hate me."

From the corner of my eye, I see Aridam pick up his mate and rush from the cellar. I worry for the little human, but this situation is my priority. I can't let anyone kill my mate, even if he deserves it. I repeat my question. "Ivan! Are you hurt?" My tone is sharp.

He flinches at my voice, and I pause, unsure. "I won't harm you." He gives a small shake of his head. No injuries, then. His voice is still soft, not matching the image I have of him in my mind. Is he acting?

"Zhenechka. My name is Zhenechka Morozov." Confusion flows through me. I'll get an explanation later, but right now I need to get him settled.

"Do you know what I am to you, Zhenechka?"

"*Da*. Um, I'm a little . . . a little confused. I think you're my soul mate. I can see your soul reaching for mine . . . but why? I thought I lost my chance at a mate when I was turned?"

He saw my what? Never mind. I might not have any answers for him, but I can find out who does. I'd like to know what the fuck is going on myself.

"We'll figure this out later. Right now, we need to get you situated. Do you want to stay here?" I know everyone else followed Ari and Rhys through the portal, so it's safe for him to stay for now. He doesn't answer, just a slight widening of his eyes as he takes in my demon form. I don't see fear in his gaze, so I let him peruse. His lips part slightly, and a pretty pink tongue peeks out to glide over his full bottom lip. Since we're the only ones here, I assume it will be safe to be in my more vulnerable human form, and my mate doesn't seem to have registered my appearance until now, as shocked as he is, but I don't trust him enough for that.

I think back to the last time I really looked at my demon form in the mirror. Yellow-tinted skin, dark wings, almost black, with intricate designs throughout. My horns aren't nearly as large as the others', and my tail has no barbs, just a section of feather-like wisps. The feathers can turn sharp enough to cut if needed; otherwise they're just soft. The claws I'm wielding on my hands have a matching set at the top of my wings, giving me extra protection. I've been speaking around my fangs for long enough that I don't sound that much different in either form.

"How can I stay here? No one will come to try to claim it?"

"I don't know, Zhenechka. I can ask about our options in a little bit. First, do you actually want to stay here, or is there somewhere else you'd like to go?"

27

His eyes are still shiny with tears and confusion. He shrugs.

"Okay, you'll stay here, then. If you change your mind at any time, say something. I refuse to do something without your consent." I won't abandon him yet even though I want nothing to do with him. My dick isn't quite on the same page; I've been hard since I realized who he was. Neither his tears nor my disgust over his morals have stemmed the flow of arousal. If anything, his stuttered breathing and vulnerability just fueled it. I maneuver us back up the stairs, past the sea of pink, and into the only slightly less wretched blue room. He follows me without protest, and I can't help but find it both odd and endearing. He stills when we pass the symbols slightly visible on the back of the door, and I raise my eyebrow in question.

"I wanted to make sure someone would know we had been here if no one saved him in time."

"What does it say?"

"*Pomogite.* It's Russian for 'help us' . . . or it's as close as I could get it by using a butter knife. This is an old cottage; the wood is very dry, so it splits easily. Normally I wouldn't have been able to do even this. I couldn't do anything that had the potential to harm Constantine or those in his care for any reason, so having an unauthorized weapon would have been against the rules."

His words imply he tried at some point, though. The biggest question I have is why would he help that shit-stain of a vampire in the first place?

"How long have you been with Constantine, Zhenechka?"

"Please, call me Zhen. To answer your question, a little over twenty years." He looks away, out the window.

Twenty years. Twenty fucking years he's been that sicko's lackey. "He was your sire?"

"Correct."

"How was he controlling you? Normally a sire's compulsion on their younglings is only effective—"

"For a few hours at most, yes. I'm aware." His sharp tone confuses me more. He's been so docile up until now. His intimidating stature and looks are a contradiction to his soft voice and sweet eyes, but I cannot let his sweet demeanor distract me from getting answers.

"So, how?"

"I'm really tired. Can I lie down now?"

I know he's evading my question, but why? Things aren't adding up. I want to believe his scared kitten act, but he's hiding so much. I feel edgy and restless. Unsettled.

"Of course. I'll get that update while you rest." I need to find out what my mate is trying to hide from me, and check on the little human he's responsible for torturing.

Zhen

The demon's footsteps grow quieter, leaving me to my thoughts. He was beautiful in his full form. I'll admit I haven't met many demons, so I don't even know what kind he is. I wonder if his other, human-like form will match his demon coloring. I assume so based on his facial structure and eyes. They're a blue so dark they seem black. Blue doesn't seem to fit the rest of his demon coloring, so I attribute it to his human form. A hypothesis I can test later.

I curl up on the bed. I wasn't being untruthful when I said I was tired. I'm twenty years of tired. Exhaustion is taking the edge off my panic, and I couldn't be more grateful. I have no idea what comes next . . . if there even *is* a next.

There's no way I'll come away from this unscathed. I tortured that human within an inch of his life. Heartbroken, I watched his soul bonds fade, but I couldn't utter a sound. I had tried so hard to fight the compulsion, to no avail. I carved Constantine's symbol into the human's skin while the older vamp watched gleefully, knowing it hurt me to do it. I couldn't fight the command to drink from the human's unconscious body even though I was unable to keep it down once I was alone. The boost his blood gave me for that short period was enough to help me resist the smallest compulsions, like hesitating for a second when given a command, and it allowed me to carve the symbols into the door, but nothing else.

I was weak, a failure. My father would be so disappointed in me. He'd expected his children to be strong and just. To hold no quarter even unto ourselves. In my place, he would have succeeded in killing himself after the transformation. I failed at that too. Constantine laughed at my attempt, calling me foolish and weak. He wasn't wrong.

I am aware that I'm spiraling, that the evidence points to my thoughts being irrational. The scientist in me is appalled, but I cannot control my mind anymore. For the longest time it was the only control I had, but now that the compulsion is gone, my sense of everything has shattered. I don't know how to make simple decisions anymore after having been told what to do for twenty years. I'm free, so why do I feel so lost?

I let sleep claim me, knowing my troubles will still be there when I wake up.

A slamming door jolts me fully awake. I haven't felt this rested in years. I check my watch and realize the late hour. Fuck, I'm going to be late! I swing my feet over the edge of the bed and am halfway across the room before the events of today catch up to me. My head spins, reminding me I haven't had blood. I stand as still as possible with my hand resting on the foot of the garish bed, waiting for the dizziness to abate. After a while I'm only a little woozy, but it seems manageable for now.

The branded door swings open, and I know instinctively that the enraged man standing in its opening is my mate. Face red and eyes wild, his blond hair plastered to his forehead. He's beautiful even in his fury, but my mind is scrambling to figure out why he's aiming his anger at me. I haven't done anything in the time he's been gone, have I? I don't get far in my wondering before he unleashes his anger, forcing me to step back as he stalks forward.

"He DIED! That human you cut to pieces fucking died in his mate's arms." His chest heaves. "AND I WASN'T THERE! I wasn't there for his mate, for my team. I was *here* with YOU! How can I stand there and tell the people closest to me, my *family*, that my fucking MATE is responsible for killing one of theirs? Fuck! No! No, I won't do it. I—"

He chokes on his words, voice cracking. I know what's coming. Dread swirls through my gut. I open my mouth to explain, to beg him to give me a chance. He pushes forward with a new look of determination before any words can escape my dry mouth.

"I, Azvameth, reject you, Zhenechka Morozov, as my mate."

I knew it was coming, but I still feel his rejection like a physical blow. My knees buckle, and the air whooshes out of me. I brace my hands on the floor in front of me, trying to hold back my scream. I deserve this. I'm a monster. Oh, Rhys, I'm so sorry.

Continuing to spiral won't change the outcome. My weakness allowed my mate to lose his friend. When I can catch my breath, I finally respond.

"I never wished to hurt him. I didn't have a choice. I'm so sorry." Oh hell, this hurts. I dare to look up. His face is blank, eyes dead. I can feel him detaching from me, so I peek at his soul. He is in so much pain he practically pulses with it.

I did this to him. Perhaps not intentionally, but it's because of me that he's breaking apart, so it's only fitting that I help ease that pain. Not being connected to his friend's murderer would definitely be a start. I gather my pain and push it aside as best I can, forcing myself to choke out my truth.

"I understand, Azvameth. I-I hope one day you find the mate you deserve." One more deep breath. "I, Zhenechka Morozov, accept your rejection."

Pain flashes in his soul, but no movement or inkling of feeling shows in his face before he turns and strides from the room without another word, leaving the door open. I don't move from the ground, just curl up into a pathetic ball and let the grief consume me. Our bond never completed, so there was no actual bond to sever. It will just be painful until one of us passes or we take a new mate . . . fated or otherwise.

Tomorrow. I'll pick myself up tomorrow.

Chapter Three

Zhen

I am a scientist. I can do this. Organization and lists will help shape my new world. I try to push away the unease I have for being in a house that holds so many painful memories, but I have nowhere else to go.

I look through the desk in the farmhouse, gathering any scrap of paper and every writing utensil I can find. After upending each drawer and cabinet in the living room, I move to the kitchen and repeat the process. The papers slowly pile up, and the various pens and pencils give me comfort.

Once satisfied with my haul, I bring them all into the dining room. There's little to no furniture in the house on the main floor, so I spread everything out on the worn hardwood flooring under an old light fixture, where the sun coming in from the large bay windows bathes the area in a soft golden light.

I found a half-empty notebook earlier, much to my delight, so I pick that up first and title the last page with today's date. I've always used notebooks backward. I don't know why, but having my most recent work visible first settles something in me. The process of writing down everything that needs done is soothing, familiar.

I continue to write until my hand cramps. The tasks are not organized yet, but I can figure that out later. A few of these I can take care of starting now, so I put a tick mark next to the two I feel comfortable tackling today.

- See if my hybrid body will accept animal blood in place of human or supernatural.
- Draw three vials of my blood and test T-cell levels. One now, one after consumption, and one twenty-four hours later.

I will have to rummage through the remaining medical supplies Constantine allowed me to keep here. I know there's enough for blood drawing and storing since his plan was to restock our supply for more testing. Hopefully those testing materials are here too. I add "find more medical supplies" to my short list and stand up, feeling a bit dizzy. It's been five days since I consumed the demon mate's Null blood.

I know from past experience three days is my comfort zone, so I need to test my old bloodlust theorics as quickly as possible so I don't die before I can move on to my new one.

My primary purpose now is to help the ones I harmed under Constantine's command and take down the angel who helped him. The only memory I have of meeting him hits me.

"Why would you bring him, Constantine?"

"He's not going to be able to tell anyone anything, so why should it matter? You worry about your own people while I worry about mine."

The angel just grunts in response. His soul is dark, heavy with sin and malice. If I could shudder I would. He gives me the creeps.

"There are three we won't be saving or needing any longer. Do you want them or should we just wait for them to die?"

"Let me see them." We walk to the cellar, and a witch meets us in front of the door. She waves her hand, and we can see through it. The supernaturals huddle together, but it doesn't stop me from looking at their souls. I assume that's what the angel is doing, too, because we come to the same conclusion.

"There is only one worth having right now. I'll take her, the fae girl. The other two I will shred as payment for her."

"Agreed."

The angel enters the room and pulls the fae from her crouched position, talking softly. She willingly embraces him, tears of relief falling down her face. I wish I could scream at her that it's all a trick. That his soft smile and charming looks are all lies. He looks like a fairy-tale prince. High born angel as he is, he's hiding his evil in plain sight, and apparently he's very, very good at it.

The nameless angel pulls the fae into his arms and touches their foreheads together. She is knocked out immediately, but to the other two, it looks like she's just sleeping peacefully. He sets her down and walks confidently over to the shifters. One wolf and one bear, if I'm remembering correctly. He reaches toward both of them, and they let him approach before he plunges his hands into their chests and rips their souls partially from their bodies with a roar. With some effort, he keeps hold with one hand, raking the nails of his other through their eyes, ripping their souls' tongues out, and twisting their fingers completely off. He's maiming them so they cannot report what they've witnessed to a place they've called "Reception."

The angel's last move is to rip a few strips of their soul completely away from their bodies, letting their bodies drop into heaps on the floor. He inspects the large strips, smiles malevolently, and consumes them, going as far as to lick his fingers afterward.

His gaze connects with Constantine's before they exchange nods. He picks up the still-unconscious fae and simply disappears.

I steady myself against the pale-yellow wall while coming out of the flashback. It takes another moment to clear my head and start toward the big pantry. That's where Constantine had me stash the supplies while the human . . . Rhys, while Rhys was unconscious. I find the box I had haphazardly thrown things into while rushing to get away from the estate. The cardboard is smashed in a few places where it had fallen in the SUV. I gently pick it up and place it on a shelf in front of me, moving a few jars of what might be food in the process.

Peering inside the box, I find a beaker has broken. The glass is in larger chunks, so it's not everywhere, but I still take extra care when removing the microscope and box of vials. The needles, slides, and tubes are lying at the bottom. I pluck out a few of each and grab an elastic band. Holding them in my right hand, I snag the microscope with my left. Arms now full, I wander back to my piles of paper and arrange a little workspace in front of the large windows. It only takes a second to tie off the elastic and locate a good vein on the inside of my left elbow.

Shit. I forgot the alcohol wipes. Leveraging myself back to standing, I quickly grab the rest of the supplies I need.

Okay, deep breath. I only need to stick myself once, but twisting the tube one-handed while keeping the needle and tube holder steady is harder than I anticipated. It takes longer than I'm used to, but once the tube is full, I pull the needle out and set it aside. I remove a small amount of blood from the tube with the syringe I grabbed and place a single drop onto the slide. Once the slide is under the microscope, I watch how the cells behave. I reach for a scrap paper and jot down the date and time, along with my observations. I have protein-energy malnutrition, PEM. The results are definitive; it's the same as someone who is quickly starving. My stomach doesn't growl, but I do feel empty.

On to phase two. I head outside to try to hunt an animal. At least I know what I'm doing in this regard. My family believed in living off the land as much as possible, but respecting life. I won't need a weapon other than my fangs and bare hands, so I don't worry about grabbing the rifle I can see leaning against the railing on the back porch. Gazing into the trees, I narrow my vision and open my senses, searching for blood. Large game is about a mile away, so I take off in that direction, trying not to make a sound. Something else I'll need to practice. I have speed, but my stealth needs work. Pain slices through my chest, reminding me of my mate's anguished words. I shake off the feeling, knowing I did the right thing by letting him go.

I see the large buck and feel a twinge of guilt that I'll be killing him, but I embrace the hunger and let it take over. I slam into the animal and waste no time, striking his neck. I use my hands to hold him to me, not allowing him to move at all from the chest up. The first mouthful is disgusting, and I try not to gag. I choke down another few gulps before my stomach starts to rebel. It's so gross. Yucky isn't an adult description, but that's the taste. Like the vegetable you hate most as a puree, but with a side of hair.

I use my hands to break the twitching buck's neck. I want to use the meat to see if I can supplement missing nutrients with any kind of human food. Vampires don't need to eat, getting all they need from blood, but I'm not just a vampire. Perhaps part of my deficiency is due to my lack of real food. I need to add another vial draw to the list. That's four more draws. I hope I have enough supplies.

I drag the buck back toward the house, feeling a bit stronger but incredibly nauseous. Maybe this is a placebo effect or simple desperation, but I need this to work. Finding a tree with a sturdy low-hanging branch, I dump the deer and go searching for some rope and a knife. While inside, I do my second draw.

While I wait for the animal to drain completely of blood into the bucket I got from the cellar, I complete my next task. I refuse to stay inside the cellar for any period of time. The smell of old blood and decay paired with memories means I would rather rig up the deer against the tree than use the hooks installed originally for that purpose. The rope gives me leverage anyway since I'm weaker than I should be right now.

I sit cross-legged on the ground, my back to the house, and try to focus only on my breathing. In slowly to the count of five, out for five. In, out. I repeat until my mind is clear. I take stock of my body, tapping into the magic just sitting in my abdomen, and reacquainting myself. My magic is half of what it used to be, and I keenly feel the loss of the elemental side of me. I need to nurture the magic I have, stretch it like a muscle that is no longer bound. Since no other people are here, I cannot really do anything with my soul sight, but I can connect and watch it while meditating each night.

With a wince I realize I've meditated much longer than I thought and need to test the blood I drew earlier before it's too late.

It's not enough. I can tell by the low T cells that the animal blood alone won't sustain me. There was barely any improvement—the equivalent to a teaspoon of regular blood. I haven't gotten to the part of my list to figure out how to get my hands on bagged blood. It requires contacts I don't have. I swallow down the despair threatening to choke me.

No, I need to make a meal. I grab a mystery jar from the pantry and head outside with a lone pot I found buried under a random pile in the kitchen earlier. I'll try to cook the meat in it first since I preferred it that way before my transformation, but I need to try to eat it all cold and raw at some point to measure any difference.

There's no power or water in the cottage, so I'm racing against the setting sun to get my fire started. I can see just fine in the dark, but I may not be the biggest predator out here, and the smell of the deer will attract more wildlife. I don't feel like fending off wolves or bears if I don't need to. I need to preserve the strength I have left; testing myself physically wasn't exactly the best idea if I can't restore the energy I used.

With an old-fashioned flint, I light my fire in the pile of twigs I saw lying around the yard. The pot warms up quickly, so I throw a few chunks of meat in, searing the sides. Once it's done, I pop the lid on the jar and take a sniff. Peaches and cinnamon? I test it, preparing to hate it like I did the blood.

Huh, not bad. I throw a peach in the pot to get it warm. Grilled fruit was always a favorite of mine before. I try it again now. Eh, it was better cold. The meat stops sizzling, and I check it. I pull the pot off the fire, deeming it done, and flinch at the heat the pot is giving off. I have to use my hands, so I try to pull it apart as quickly as possible.

The meat isn't terrible, and the jar of peaches is gone. I wasn't a fan after the first few bites, but I forced myself to finish it. Even though I didn't like doing it, I'm not fighting to keep it down like I was the blood. Unfortunately the effort has probably been wasted since I don't feel any different; I'll see how the testing goes in about an hour before I let go of the hope I have for meat being the answer to my blood problem. I clean up, not wanting to leave traces of the meal outside.

I unhook the deer and drag its carcass about a mile away from the cottage, picking my way over fallen branches. I can't preserve the meat, so I hope an animal finds it before it rots. I make a note to myself that if I need to hunt again, smaller game is better since I won't need the blood.

I haven't uttered a word today, but the general silence doesn't bother me. I'm used to not speaking for days on end. I think the longest I've gone without making a sound is a couple months, years ago. I was never to make a sound unless told to, which was incredibly rare. I only interacted with Constantine and a few of his acquaintances. More in the past two years than in the previous ten. That's how long ago this plan was hatched.

I know very few names, but I remember each of their faces . . . and each of their souls. I remember which people wanted to be there and which were being forced or coerced. Only a couple were compelled. The rest were just disgusting creatures putting power above their own people's lives.

I repeat the blood-drawing process for the third time, recording everything I find. Still not enough. It helped more than the blood, but the cell count is nowhere near healthy for any supernatural. I close my eyes, tears of frustration building behind my lids. I refuse to accept that my only options are hurting a human or tracking down a blood bank and raiding it. They're always guarded, and it would be more trouble than it's worth, and I would end up having to harm the humans anyway. I have no compulsion. That ability apparently did not take during my transformation. It's a good trade-off in order to keep my soul sight, but I'm despairing it now.

I roll my eyes, chastising myself for wallowing in self-pity. Things could be worse. I need some sleep. I'll figure out more tomorrow. I head back to the blue room, gathering the pillow that I'm pretending has traces of Azvameth's scent against my nose and breathing it in. I don't blame him for rejecting me; it was the logical decision. I just wish I could have met him before all this, when I was worth having.

Chapter Four

Azvameth

I've been drowning my pain by tracking Constantine's known coven members, the ones we didn't find at the main estate the night of Rhys's kidnapping. I've tracked every single one down and have gotten as much information out of them as possible about the rescued and damaged souls and the coven leader's overall plan. Which is zilch. His own members are clueless, just taking the blood given to them by their leader and reaping the benefits of suped-up blood. They were under the impression it was freely given. Idiots. I need to check in with the team, but I can't bring myself to turn on my cell. I'd texted Astaroth my game plan for the interrogations before immediately shutting down my phone so at least someone knew what I was doing.

I shouldn't care; I shouldn't be obsessing about Zhenechka. It's my sin. The one time I'm counting on apathy and it has left the building. My chest is caving in with the pain of rejecting my mate. I won't say I regret it, but I'm blinded by emotion every time my mind touches the frail space where the bond should be residing.

I head back to the team house in Hell long enough to swipe clothing from my room. I need to hurry if I want to make it to my spot while it's still light out. My portal opens to my safe space—the butterfly garden in Florida. It's the largest in the world, housing enough of the beautiful creatures to entertain me for hours. Each one is perfectly unique.

My fascination with them started at a young age. I stumbled across a neglected state park while ditching Allocer's training for the day. I'd grasped portals quickly, ahead of others my age. I'd only been around eight when I could portal to the mortal realm without fear. I ditched because I was bored. While walking one of the overgrown trails, I saw a viceroy butterfly. I rushed to catch up to it, disturbing the foliage. It spooked the dainty thing, so I stilled. I waited for the butterfly to get used to my presence before I moved again at a much slower pace. I sat on a fallen log and just watched.

Their wings weren't at all like mine. Huge compared to their bodies but whisper thin. Their control was astounding. Hours passed as I sat. It was the most at peace I'd ever felt, my hands not twitching in impatience even once. I was getting ready to head back, when one landed on my upturned hand while it was resting on my knee. I held my breath as another landed on my wing. I'd always preferred my demon form, so I was in it as much as possible. After another few minutes, a dozen butterflies graced me. They flew away after a while, but the feeling never left.

Now, I come here to think. I don't reveal my form to humans; I know better. The yellow of my demon skin attracts butterflies, but I cannot risk it in public. I sit on one of the many available benches and watch them, waiting for the peace to wash over me. My chest aches. Footsteps to my left indicate I'm not alone, but I don't look toward the sound.

"Ahh, I thought I might find you here." Astaroth's voice washes over me.

"Fucking Belial," I grumble.

"Do not blame him, Azvameth. He did not reveal your hobby flippantly." He slides gracefully into the empty space next to me. The bench creaks under our combined weight.
We sit in silence for a few moments before I say something. "Not to sound like an ass, but why are you here?"

"You cut yourself off from the team, from me. It's unacceptable, my demon." He almost says it like "my child," sending a tendril of warmth through me.
"There are developments you are unaware of. It's been entirely too long since you've gone dark. I've given you the time you seemed to need, but it ends now."
I blow out a breath, steeling myself. "How is Aridam?"

His hesitation is telling. "We cannot discuss it here; care to join me in my office?" Oh hell, it's bad. I don't want to hear what he has to say, but his question was not actually a request. His tone was commanding.

"Of course." I stand, and we walk toward the exit, passing children whose faces reflect the same awe mine did and haggard parents looking after them. Humanity has a lot of drawbacks, but a natural want to protect your kids is certainly not one of them. Parents in Hell are awful for the most part, for obvious reasons.

We head to the side of the building, avoiding the parking lot. The second we are alone, Astaroth disappears, leaving me to portal to his office alone. I'm sorely tempted to just go back inside, to ignore the summons.

With gritted teeth I force my feet through my own portal and stop on the Main Street of Hell. The office is a minute's walk away, giving me time to rehearse my defense for not killing Zhenechka. I rejected him, which has to be enough.

As I pass Stazie, I have the passing thought of using her or just sex in general as an escape from the pain, but my stomach roils violently at the mere thought. I hate that I had even entertained the idea of it, though I wouldn't be cheating on Zhenechka. The thought feels like ash in my mouth, and my dick actually tried to crawl back inside my body, so it definitely wasn't on board anyway.

Franco is sitting at his desk right outside Astaroth's office. He spots me and waves me in, giving a sympathetic smile.

The black desk in Astaroth's office has been there for as long as I can remember. It's comforting, the simple things that never change while my life has been turned upside down. My Duke of Hell sits behind it, staring off to the side. He rolls his shoulders as I plop down onto the plush office chair opposite him.

"Now. Let's get a few things sorted before I explain what happened here while you were gathering info. What did you find?"

"I didn't get anything useful; all were uninformed or too simple to ask questions past their orders."

"I need you to explain everything anyway. Humor me."

I go over every coven member and their story in detail. I almost gloss over the info I tried to gather about Zhen, but I won't lie to my duke over a misguided loyalty.

"Who is Zhenechka? I thought you were working on questioning Ivan?"

My throat squeezes and my chest burns with the effort to hold back my entire story. "Ivan's real name is Zhenechka, if we are to believe him."

"Why would we not believe him? According to Aridam, he was being compelled."

"That's impossible; he's been turned for twenty years. No sire can keep another vampire under compulsion for twenty years or compel one who's already that old."

"Not impossible. Unheard of, but not impossible." I scoff as he goes on. "It would explain a lot of his behavior while Rhys was captive."

"How would we know his behavior? It's not like Belial hacked some camera footage."

"We will get to that in a second. I'm trying to gauge how much this Zhenechka would know about Constantine's operation if the coven leader had him under compulsion. Perhaps everything. I want to speak with him immediately."

I grit my teeth. "Understood, sir."

"Where did you leave him?"
"At the farmhouse we found R-Rhys at." My voice cracks on the human's name.

"How much blood did you leave him with? Enough for a week? Two?" I feel all my own blood rush from my face. Astaroth notices my face blanch and scowls. "You left a young vampire with no blood? At that age they need to feed every other day to be comfortable. Assuming he's still there and not hunting in the nearest town, he's going to be ravenous. Dammit, Azvameth!"

"I-I wasn't. I didn't think . . ." Shame swamps me. I need to go now to make sure he's okay, but I can't get my legs to work before Astaroth continues.

"I will bring some when I visit. Now, on to my piece. You need to sit and listen." I give an impatient nod. I'm struggling to focus on anything but Zhen.

"Rhys did indeed die, but to make a long story short, Michael allowed him to appeal his death, and he won." My gasp doesn't make him miss a beat. "He is currently with the team at the witch Lily's shop . . . resting. We met with him and got his rendition of

49

what happened while he was captive. His soul is not whole; he gave up a piece to return, so we do need to monitor how that affects his interactions with the team going forward. Kieran seems to have an interesting effect on him." He smirks.

"He's alive?"

"Yes, Azvameth. Which you would have known if you hadn't turned off your phone."

Reality crashes into me. "Oh God. No. NO!" I can't breathe. I rejected my mate because he had killed the human. *He still tortured him.* He was under compulsion. *The whole time? Impossible.* Astaroth said not impossible. I didn't ask! *He avoided my questions.* Yeah, because I was so welcoming and trustworthy. What have I done? My thoughts are battling as I sit frozen.

"Azvameth. I will allow you more time to process, take all the time you need, but I need to check on the young vampire and the intact souls."

"He's my mate." It's a devastated whisper.

"Who?" His gaze is intense; I cannot look him in the eye.

"Zhenechka Morozov. I-I rejected him when Rhys died. Astaroth, I—Oh God." A sob tears out of me, starting the process of me completely losing my shit.

"Oh, Azvameth. Your impulsiveness may have once again broken something you might not be able to fix. First we need to make sure your mate is still there. We can only hope he hasn't gone in search of food of the human variety . . . It's been days." He stands and steps away from his desk, poking his head out to talk to Franco. I hear very little, only catching "Morozov" before Astaroth turns his attention back to me.

"Let's go. I'll head there first to try to smooth things over. Pick up two weeks' worth of blood from the stores in Louisiana and meet me at the farmhouse when you're done. And for hell's sake, check your phone." He stares me down, and I can feel the disappointment from here. "I would punish you for keeping things from me *again*, but I believe you will be doing plenty of that on your own. If he's from the family I believe he is, that will explain a great deal . . . both for you and the souls we have been trying to help. Start thinking of ways to grovel, my dear demon. You're going to need them."

It's taken longer than I'd hoped to get to the blood bank we use in New Orleans. The locals don't ask many questions, and the city is home to a dense population of humans who are aware of supernaturals. We've always had a bigger foothold in the French Quarter than we have anywhere else in the south. Vegas is the next largest. As I wait at the drop point for our witchy contact, I finally turn on my phone. It goes crazy, vibrating non-stop for a solid minute. I check voicemails first, deleting them as I listen. The message is the same, only varying slightly. "Where are you?" and "Rhys is alive!" I open texts to see more of the same, until I reach Belial's message in our group chat.

Belial: *Hey, Rhys asked for me to take pictures instead of having everyone ask to look at him "like an animal at the zoo." He wants to just move on. No one is to bring the pictures or their contents up to him.*

Attached are the images. Some are close-ups of vicious bites on what looks like his hip and neck. Next show the meticulous cuts on his legs. The last few pictures of his neck, chest, and back make me nauseous. I feel vomit crawling up my throat and fight to keep it down.

Zhen did this. Not all of it, I'm sure, but he participated in the horror I'm looking at. The emblem carved into Rhys's back is huge, taking up over half his back. The scarring is messy in places, giving the lines an even more jagged appearance. His neck shows someone had tried to rip the Null's mating mark from his skin completely. His body is one big bruise. A kaleidoscope of colors highlight his body.

I lose it. I vomit in the bushes of Woldenberg Park, emptying my stomach completely. I have tortured beings for information, and I've enjoyed it immensely, so I don't know why I'm so hung up on this. The goal was to make him suffer as much as possible. I know Zhen was under compulsion for at least part of this, but how do I use that to justify his actions when the results are in front of me clear as day? Maybe I'm freaking out because I care for the Null. A little.

A pretty blonde saunters by me, dropping her purse at my feet. I'm startled enough to flinch, which never happens.

"This is the best we could do. Six bags. Should give a young vampire two weeks if they're careful. We can have more ready in a few weeks." She doesn't wait for a reply, just turns her back to me and skips off. Ballsy.

I know I need to gather the bags and head out, but I need just another minute to steady myself. The images fight for dominance in my mind. I need to look again, make sure I'm not missing anything.

There are pinprick marks, like a cleaner bite. They are sparse but still surrounded by bruising. I try to determine which ones are Zhenechka's but cannot figure it out.

I still feel sick, but I no longer doubt my ability to walk. I trudge back toward the alley I portaled in from, only to find a couple using it for a quickie. This goes on for a few blocks before I find an empty one.

The purse full of blood bags is getting warmer. I need to hurry.

Chapter Five

Zhen

Using the morning light, I sort and prioritize my task lists. A big one for today is to record everything relevant to what happened to my family and everything I know about Constantine's plan and associates. I understand my hand will cramp when I'm writing the letters to the relevant people I think can help, but I do have a voice recorder and extra tapes I found in the pink room earlier today while searching for more paper. This needs to get done as soon as possible. My voice may need breaks from overuse, but I can talk until it's gone.

I've run out of tubes. I would like to take a few more samples, but the evidence is pointing to my inability to forego fresh or at least bagged blood. The other food and testing have given me extra time, but I will either starve or go feral within the next day.

I press record on the machine, wanting to get the stories out before the battery dies or I run out of time. I clear my throat a few times to warm up my voice.

"My name is Zhenechka Morozov, and I believe I am the last of the Morozov Coven. According to my research, I may also be the last soul mage . . ."

Sometime later, I feel a disturbance in the air, and I know immediately that I'm not alone. The presence doesn't feel like Azvameth, but it's close. Probably demon. Maybe it's the mate of Rhys. The wrath demon wanted to kill me even before his mate died. I cannot imagine how much he must want my blood on his hands now. I flick the recorder off, not wanting my death to be immortalized forever.

"I'm almost done recording. If you could please wait to kill me until I have successfully shared what I know, I would appreciate it. I know you do not owe me any reprieve, demon, but I would be thankful all the same."

The serious-looking stranger is not who I was expecting. His reddish-brown hair is cropped short on the sides, a little longer on top. His green eyes are dark enough to be black in places. How fascinating. I have not seen him before, but I've heard whispers of the Dukes of Hell being able to teleport instead of using portals. "Ah, I seem to be mistaken. You are a duke, correct?"

"Correct, Zhenechka. My name is Astaroth."
"Interesting. Are you here to kill me, Astaroth?"

"Not at all. There have been a lot of misunderstandings lately, and I would like to address them."

"Perfect. Communication is key and all that. I really must finish this recording, but maybe we can discuss these misunderstandings afterward? I believe I only have about an hour of voice left; I would hate to waste it."

"By all means, please do." He makes himself comfortable on the floor beside me, and it strikes me as humorous. A duke sitting on the floor like a common person. I hold back a giggle, finding this significantly funnier than I would normally.

"You wouldn't happen to have any bagged blood, would you? I am unraveling, I believe."

"Some will be arriving shortly with your mate."

Pain stabs me. "Not my mate, but I appreciate the offer of blood. I'm not too proud to take it. I will turn feral soon without it; we are on day six, after all."

"I'm so sorry, Zhenechka. We—"

"*Nyet*. I must record this while my mind is still intact. You will put me down before I go completely feral, though, yes? It's a kindness I don't deserve, but I will beg if I have to." I don't wait for him to reply before I press record and start talking.

"Constantine D'arius met with four people regularly. They were the key parts of his master plan; they kept everything running smoothly. Alpha Gregory of the Albany pack; Italy's coven leader, Felicity Bianchi; greed demon Orobas; and the angel. I don't know his name. I believe it starts with 'Ab,' but that's based on a slip-up from Constantine before he corrected himself."

A hand moving into my field of vision startles a yelp from me. I must have blocked the demon duke out. I stop the recording.

"Are you sure of that name? Orobas?"

"*Da*, of course."

"Excuse me, please." He disappears and reappears within a minute. "Sorry about that. I had to relay a message to my assistant. He will round up Orobas and his team for questioning."

I nod. Reasonable. He cannot go on my word alone. A fresh wave of dizziness hits me, and I close my eyes, placing my head in my hands to try to steady the spinning.

"Zhenechka, are you okay?"

"Sorry, yes, just a dizzy spell." I force my eyes open and give him my best interpretation of a smile.

"You need to eat."

"I'll be okay. I can wait until Azvameth drops off the blood."

"No. You will feed now. I won't allow you to take too much, but you need it now." He thrusts his wrist toward my face.

"I could get a glass—ompf!"

He shoves his wrist into my mouth, cutting off my offer to not bite him. My body reacts before I can protest, my fangs sinking into his supple skin. I draw in the first mouthful and whimper. His blood is potent and so, so good. Behind my eyes burn as I taste the difference between blood forced and blood freely given. It makes a difference, for this to be given freely. For once I don't feel sick; I feel energized. I continue at a steady pace, refusing to allow myself to drain more than I should.

An enraged growl sounds from across the room, freezing me mid-swallow. A gentle hand cups the back of my head and smooths it, like petting a cat. "Relax, Zhenechka, take what you need. He can wait." Astaroth's tone is soft, comforting.

I pull in two more mouthfuls before my mind settles and my body quiets.

"Thank you," I whisper as I wipe my mouth on my sleeve. I don't want to look over at Azvameth. I can feel the disgust and anger in his stare. "I, um, have a few more things to record, if you don't mind? I know now that I won't starve, but it will still be helpful to have all of my information in one place with a way to share it with those who need it."

"Of course, Zhenechka. Your view has been invaluable so far." I nod, still avoiding looking to where I know Azvameth is standing.

I press record once again. "The meetings I attended gave me very little information outside of my own observations. From what I gathered, Constantine tested and sampled the blood with my assistance. Felicity gathered non-shifter supernaturals and dropped off their blood to Constantine for us to test. Gregory supplied his shifters as blood slaves in exchange for money and territory. The angel, he . . . he took some of the stronger or purer souls with him when he left, so I have no idea what he did with them. The . . . he, um, shredded most of the remaining souls of the supernaturals so they could not disclose what happened to them after they died. Some already close to death . . . he *consumed* them. I cannot fathom why, but I saw him physically eat parts of their souls.

"I want to make it very clear that I did not infer this information. It is not a theory. I am a soul mage; I can see every person's soul and interpret its behavior. I'm not trained, as no one could know of my existence. My brother was a death mage, or more commonly called a necromancer since we were hiding as witches. I learned a lot through sitting in during his lessons." My voice wavers, and I pause the recording.

"I know you have many questions. Would you like to ask them now before we discuss the miscommunications? I believe my voice will fail soon, so I will have to whisper." It's a gross understatement.

My throat burns, and every word is raw and filled with pain.

"You can rest, Zhenechka. You've had quite the past few days." Astaroth's tone is soothing.

"No thank you. I would like to answer them for you now, please, and call me Zhen."

"So polite. I heard a great deal of your recording. Would you mind letting me listen to it in its entirety?"

"Of course you may listen. There are multiple. I made the recordings primarily for your team and its contacts. I knew you would have better luck stopping them than I do."

Astaroth nods. "Are these things answered in your recordings: How did you come to be with Constantine, how did you keep your mage abilities if you were turned, and why does compulsion work on you?"

"Yes, no, and no. The first was relevant, but the last two are purely about me so I saw no point. I have no idea how I kept my abilities intact. It might have to do with which types of mage I am, or was. Elemental and soul. A dual mage is rare enough, so I'm assuming it was too much for the transformation to eradicate. Compulsion works because I am not all vampire. I can eat solid food with no adverse effects, so there's a tradeoff."

Silence blankets the room, and it's awkward enough that I just shove the recorder in his direction. "You can make copies, and if you have more questions, you know where to find me. I believe it's time for the communication discussion, but I do have a request or two, if that's acceptable?"

"And what would those be?" His head tilts to the side, and he studies me as he tucks the recorder into his suit jacket.

"If I could gain access to medical supplies? I have an ongoing study I wish to continue. It's not the one Constantine had me working on, I assure you."

"What is it focusing on, then?" He sounds intrigued but wary. Understandable.

"How different foods and levels of blood affect my T-cell levels. I have been able to lengthen the times between feeding due to trial and error, but I have run out of tubes and needles. I have my research here"—I point to the notebook on the floor next to me—"and long term I believe I can find the correct supplements to lengthen the time before new and transitioning vampires succumb to bloodlust. It would give them a gentler introduction into their new reality and avoid unnecessary fatalities.

"The molecular changes that occur during transformation are similar to my cellular makeup all of the time. The existence of two paranormal bodies fighting for control is impossible to evade, but the decimation of their previous supernatural identities adds a large hormonal surge that causes the bloodlust. It will take months, if not years, to develop a supplement, but I am willing to put in the work and use myself as the constant."

Astaroth simply stares at me. "You are a scientist?"

I force a chuckle. "I hold multiple PhDs, all in one scientific field or another. That is neither here nor there. Think on that request, as I do have one more, and it's a larger ask."

"I'm listening."

I glance around the room, startled to find Azvameth in human form still here, standing close to the doorway. I had assumed he left earlier. His eyes are locked on me, mixed emotions playing across his face. It shouldn't hurt that he hasn't said a word to me, but it does. I snap my gaze away from him and stare at the yellow wall of the dining room. Astaroth and I are still sitting on the floor, and I can feel my legs starting to numb.

"I would very much appreciate being allowed to meet with the supernaturals you rescued from the cells at the estate." Astaroth's shocked look is overshadowed by a furious voice from the doorway.

"Absolutely not! How could you even ask that? Compelled or not, it would be extremely traumatizing for a survivor to be forced to meet their abuser. Their worst nightmare come to life. They have been through enough! I've seen the evidence of your handiwork!" Azvameth's yell cracks against my defenses, making me flinch and look at the ground.

I clear my throat and gather the last remnants of my voice to murmur, "You're right, how careless of me. It would indeed be traumatizing to be forced to talk to someone like me after all they've been through. *Izvinite*." I clear my throat again, willing it not to give out now, standing slowly.

I direct my next statement to the demon duke who saved my life. "I will take my leave now. Thank you for listening. If you change your mind about killing me, I hope you will allow me to record the rest before doing so." I keep my back as straight as I can as I walk from the room, swiping the big satchel of blood bags on the floor in case Azvameth tries to take it back.

I hear raised voices and someone calls for me to wait, but I cannot stop or I will lose control of my emotions. If I'd known for sure that it was Astaroth, I might have stopped, but there's a chance it was Azvameth. The chance is slim, but it is indeed still a chance, so I keep walking. He can go fuck himself.

Chapter Six

Azvameth

"Wait! Zhenechka!" Astaroth sounds a little panicked. He stands and faces me. "Are you out of your mind, Azvameth?" His tone is furious.

"Why so protective of a random vampire, dear duke?" I know I'm lashing out, but I cannot find it in me to stop. I know what possessed me to shout at Zhen, but it's not a good excuse. I was filled with jealousy, and the longer he ignored me, the angrier I became. He wouldn't even look at me. "You knew I was coming with blood bags, so why the fuck did I walk in on you feeding my mate?!"

"Do you know how long he had gone without blood? SIX DAYS. He suffered because YOU did not deign to check on your own mate. You have NO leg to stand on here, Azvameth. You abused your mate and have the gall to raise your voice at me for ensuring he survived long enough to get the blood you brought?

"Do you want to know what he asked me when I showed up? He asked me to please wait until he was done recording before I killed him so he could help us take down the others responsible for all of this after he was gone. He knew he was dying and believed— probably still does—that he deserved it. He was compelled. Helpless and scared and forced to do unspeakable things. He had no choice. And you? I cannot connect who is standing in front of me to the boy I helped raise. I've never been more disappointed, Azvameth."

Astaroth levels me with his proclamation. I feel each of his words like a punch. Six days? Helpless? "What are you talking about? He was compelled the entire time?" No.

"Every minute of the last twenty years. It was torture in itself. Here." He pulls the recorder from his pocket and tosses it to me, then motions to the pile of tapes on the ground. "You need to listen to these first. Give him time to process today. I told him we would discuss some miscommunications today, and I plan to do so. He doesn't even know Rhys is alive, something I need to rectify immediately.

"You said you saw the pictures—good. Look at them again. Look at what he was forced to do. Then listen to all the recordings and check in with the team. Get yourself together while I try to salvage what I can. If he chooses to never see you again, Azvameth, you will listen." Astaroth's tone is vicious.

I set the recorder in the box with the extra tapes, pick it up to hold against my chest, and nod. I'm so jumbled up; I don't know what is happening to me. Feelings like this are new. I'm so used to being numb that I don't know how to handle any emotions deeper than surface level.

I portal back to my room in the team house where all is quiet. Venturing out into the common room, I take in the wrecked space. Deciding not to stall and ponder what caused the mayhem, I snatch a pair of Belial's extra headphones from his desk and creep back into my room. I slide onto the big black bed and grab one of my pillows, propping myself up against the headboard before carefully inserting a rubber earbud into one of my extra-sensitive ears, leaving the other dangling. I want to be able to hear if anyone shows up. I don't think I can bear seeing anyone right now. With trepidation I rewind all the tapes, knowing once I start playing one I won't want to wait to devour the rest. The last to rewind is one labeled in what I assume is Russian. Since I don't know if there's a particular order, I simply press play.

The brusque tones of my mate filter through the earbud. "My name is Zhenechka Morozov . . ." His voice is soothing even with the obvious rasp. Occasionally I pick up his stronger accent. It gets thicker the longer he talks, and I can hear the strain in his voice as he goes on. I listen intently as he describes the night vampires attacked his family, and that later he found out that he and his research were the reason for the attack. My heart aches for him as he reveals his painful transformation and the compulsion immediately imposed upon him as he woke, instead of the passing of memories that normally occurred.

On another tape, he almost glosses over the abuse he endured for twenty years. He offhandedly mentions not speaking for months, but goes into excruciating detail when he talks about how he was forced to torture various supernaturals and what tests he ran on them. The pain in his voice breaks me as he describes the ones who didn't make it. How he saw their souls leave their body, how he tried to resist the orders given to report any deaths so the souls could be "dealt with." The kindness he tried to sneak in at every opportunity. He gives the names of every person he had deduced the identity of. The sheer number of people he references is incredible for it only being a few years.

I switch tapes yet again, back to the one that was in the recorder when I started. My guilt is already eating me alive, but I press on, knowing this particular tape will gut me if it contains what I think it does.

Two streams of tears run down my face as he recounts the day Rhys was saved. How he wishes he could have done more, and his sobbing apologies to everyone he affected by not being strong enough to shake his compulsion. He switches from a scared boy to a robotic scientist multiple times. At one point he mumbles mostly in Russian, his words starting to slur. I catch the words "Constantine" and "angel" since the pronunciation is so close to English. He yelps, and the recording stutters. When he starts again, his voice is strong, and I realize this is when I was there.

He had truly not been able to wait another moment for Astaroth's blood. Fuck, I was such an irrational asshole about it. I mean, I've always known I was kind of a jerk, but this is so much worse than my normal flippancy. I was a poor excuse for a mate and acted terribly toward my boss, someone I respect, because I was jealous. Astaroth's words couldn't have been more spot on. I don't deserve my mate or my mentor. I haven't even reached out to my team.

Shit. That's one thing I can fix right now. The rest won't be fixed quickly or easily, but this is a good first step, right? I reach for my phone, pulling up Belial's contact. Pressing the call button, I know he probably won't answer. His voicemail picks up, and though I rarely leave messages, I don't want him to call back right now.

"Hey, Bel. I, um, I'm working on getting us more answers on the bigger plan. I'll be away from my phone a lot, but Astaroth is fully aware of my whereabouts. I'm glad Rhys is okay. Uh . . . bye." I sound like an idiot, but my point was made and I didn't lie. I toss my phone to the side and scoot down on my bed, staring at the ceiling.

I don't know how to reconcile all these feelings. An image of Zhen's face floats behind my now-closed eyelids. He's so striking. His features are more interesting than classically beautiful. Strong jaw, smooth face and head, perfectly proportionate nose and square chin. I've never had a type that got me going just by looks, but my body is reacting to the memory of him, to his scent. He smells like winter and a little bit of blood. Like a brisk wind, the kind that stings your lungs as you inhale, with a slight tang of copper. It's an intoxicating mix now that it no longer confuses me.

I refuse to touch my cock despite its ache. I won't use him for wanking material when I've been the cause of the pain most present on his face. My chest hasn't stopped hurting since I left, since I first walked away after his acceptance of my rash rejection. I replay his initial reaction in my mind, forcing myself to remember every hitch in his breath, the way he fell to his knees, and the devastation when I spoke. His calm façade during the rejection acceptance that I had just assumed was an admission of guilt.

Knowing what I know now, I berate myself for not listening when he tried to explain. I just want to go back and wrap him in my arms and soothe him. To have his captivating light-green eyes look at me with the same reverence they held when I first met him.

I will earn that look again. I've always cut out when things got too hard, but I won't make that mistake again. I'll fight for him; I'll fight for us until my last breath.

I startle at the sound of a slamming door. Straining to listen, I can hear someone rummaging around the kitchen. My stomach drops at the thought of seeing anyone in person right now. I scramble to check the time on my phone and curse. I've been asleep for hours, and I have a missed call from Astaroth. No voicemail, just a text asking me to call him. I call him back immediately after I portal to the same hotel room I always have reserved, begging silently for Astaroth to pick up.

"Speak." His tone is clipped.

"Hey! I mean, uh, you asked me to call?"

"Az? Okay, good. I didn't check before I answered. I just got off the phone with Aridam. Give me a second to get back to my office." I wait as patiently as possible, chewing my lip as anxiety fills me. "Still there?"

"Yeah, I'm here." I don't know where he thought I'd go when he holds the info on Zhen.

"Zhen has asked you to keep your distance for now. He's willing to work with you on tracking the members attached to the coven and the bigger players until the team is ready for an actual assignment. He will step back when they get involved; he doesn't want anyone to be uncomfortable."

"Wow, uh. Okay, I can work with that."

"I want to stress that he is willing to work with you and get to know you, but he is keeping the rejection in place. You rejected him, and he won't allow it to be swept under the rug because you feel different today than you did a few days ago. He is holding firm that the rejection remains the best decision for you." He chuckles almost fondly. A stab of jealousy hits me. "I admire him, Azvameth. His mind is a fascinating place, and I believe he'll be good for you if you both can move past the barriers you've erected."

I cannot bring myself to respond. I don't know what to think. I want to fight for us, but if he won't let me, do I respect his wishes? "What do you propose I do? You've gotten to know him a bit; as much as I hate it, I'm glad he's had someone in his corner."

"Ah, well." Another chuckle. "He means exactly what he says, Azvameth. He isn't playing a game with you. Ask him. He'll tell you what he needs from you; you just have to listen."

"When do we start? I want to respect his wish to keep distant until we start, but does he have enough blood? Does he need anything? A phone?" I could have one sent to him tonight.

"A phone might be a good idea. Make sure to give him my number."

I roll my eyes. "Fine," I grumble. A beep sounds in my ear; I lean down to check my phone.

Aridam: *Meeting is mandatory, Az.*
I ignore it for now, like I've done with every single one recently. I don't know how to interact with him anymore.

"Now, I believe you have a team meeting right now, my demon. Stop avoiding them."

Fuck.

"Yes, Dad," I say dryly. He just chuckles and hangs up.

My phone rings again almost immediately with a video chat request from Bel. I slide onto the couch in the hotel room. Has it really been so little time since I was with the demon/shifter couple in this same room? I slide to answer and plaster a bored look on my face.

"Yes, Belial?" His face has sunken a tad, and he looks exhausted.

"Where have you been? And don't give me that 'on assignment' crap. I tracked your phone because I was worried about you. You've been in the same house as me and said nothing." He can't hide his hurt.
"I will tell you, but you have to keep it to yourself for now, Bel. No, don't look offended. I'm serious. You might not like what I have to say."

"Out with it. I'm not going around spilling secrets."

"Listen until I'm done. No interrupting." He nods. I launch into a summarization. He doesn't need the full story right now. I can see his struggle to keep quiet, his face contorting a few times with his effort to hold himself back. I finish, and he lets the silence draw out.

"So, yeah. That about sums it up."

"I don't know what to say, Az. That's so fucked up." His tone is sympathetic, but I bristle.

"He's mine, Bel."

"Shut up. I mean what happened to him is fucked up. That poor man. When are you going to bring him to meet the team?"

"Are you fucking nuts? Aridam will kill him. Hell, Kek and Dev will too. I cannot see a way for me to bring him around without him getting hurt."
"What? No, Az. If you'd just talked to us, you'd know we don't blame Ivan . . . Zhen, whatever his name is. Rhys was very firm on his view of your mate. He defended him even on that first day. The only reason Rhys survived as long as he did was because of him."

"I don't know, Belial. I'll think about it." I'm not in any shape to make decisions right now.

"I'll keep my promise and keep it to myself, but you have one week. That's it. I'll tell them for you if you chicken out, got it?" I grunt in response.
"Now, we have a meeting to attend. Give me a second." I can hear him walking and see the screen travel through the team house. I hear voices but can't make out exactly what's being said.

Bel jumps in. "I hate to interrupt, but he's right, you know? I blamed you. Rhys never did. He loves us, so we need to get our heads out of our asses so we can make him happy, yeah?" His face moves to someone else. "Azvameth will video conference in, but he can't be around the team right now. He has some shit going on. I won't spill secrets, but if he doesn't enlighten the team within a week, I'll tell you all myself." I don't miss the warning glare he sends me.

"Alrighty then. Why don't you tell us why we're here, Oh Wrathful One?" I default to sarcasm so no one asks any more questions.

"Right. Okay. My mate is human. Well, human-ish. He cannot step into Hell. So we need to make a few decisions as a team about where we will reside and how the new dynamics will work . . ."

The discussion starts, and I can't help but feel hesitant to involve myself in any of the decisions. I have no idea what will happen with Zhen, so I can't weigh in.

I refocus when Belial brings up Rhys joining the team. I don't voice my denial, but I'm definitely thinking it. I wait for the envy demon's explanation. When he explains the handler idea, I know they'll cave. It's not a bad play, and if it lessens Belial's burden, I'm all for it.

We get to voting, and it's unanimous for Rhys's new position, but I cannot vote for the whole house thing. I don't even know if I'll be welcome on the team after they find out about Zhen.

"Az? Kieran? What are your concerns?" Aridam sounds so frustrated. Normally I enjoy it, but not this time.

"I will go with what the team says, but I have another . . . concern . . . at the moment. I need to wrap up this assignment, and then I'll update you all." Hopefully then I'll know what the plan is with Zhen.
"Is it personal or does it affect the team?" His question throws me. Of course he's worried about the team.

"Both, but I won't start shit until I know what's going on. It'll be fine until then. I won't let it affect you guys." I make my voice as confident as possible, but I'm lying out my ass.

"Fine. I believe Belial's warning was real. You have a week, Az. We're here if you need anything." I snort and hang up. If only he knew.

I stretch and use my phone to check how much time I have to get a phone for Zhen. I'll have to pop by the office to have Franco give me one of ours so it will still deliver messages even in Hell. I need to get going or I'll be cutting it close to when the pride demon leaves for the day.

It takes me no time at all to get ready and portal to the office. Franco smiles when I approach his desk. "Hey, Franco. Would you mind setting up a phone for me? I need to give it to someone. You can just add it to my plan."

His sly look tells me he already knows everything, but he just graciously nods and holds out his hand. "I can have it done in just a few. Want me to send it anywhere, or will you deliver it yourself, perhaps with some flowers?" His hint isn't at all subtle, and he knows it.

"I'll do it," I snarl. He smiles smugly and busies himself at his computer. I love that his desk is decked out like a mini bat cave. I may have had a small obsession with Batman when the comic first came out. An orphan meting out justice? Bet. I head out the side door to the garden, picking a variety of flowers and making a haphazard bouquet. This'll have to do.

Once the phone is good to go with the two numbers added to his contacts, I'm struck with an idea. I still have his recorder; I just need a blank tape.

Chapter Seven

Zhen

I sense Azvameth close by. I can hear his heartbeat, and the hair on the back of my neck rises. I wait for him to waltz in and ignore everything Astaroth assured me would happen. I need this time to sort through my thoughts. Alive. Rhys is alive. My relief is a physical thing, but so is the bitterness of being rejected over something that didn't happen. Correction, he died—he just didn't stay dead. I need to figure out if this changes anything, so for now I want to keep my distance from my mate. I focus on his faint heartbeat coming from the front lawn. My frustration mounts because although the conversation with Astaroth was enlightening, I'm not ready to face Azvameth yet. Movement on the porch confirms that he couldn't be bothered to listen to my plea for space.

My chest twinges, and I realize it's been too long. What is he doing? I stand from where I had set up shop in the dining area and pick my way to the door. I use the rusted peephole to see if it'll give me any clues. He gently sets something on the porch and looks almost longingly at the house before turning away. I make a mental note to look for some spray lubricant to stop the obnoxious creaking as I yank the old wooden door open, catching him on the last step with his back turned. His blond hair catches the setting sun just so, giving him an angelic look. The noise from the door must have alerted him to my presence, because he faces me, his trepidation palpable.

"What are you doing here, Azvameth? It's only been a day." Controlling my facial expressions is something I've always struggled with without compulsion, so I haven't the slightest clue what my face is doing.

"I brought you this. I know you want space and I'm trying to respect that, but I wanted you to be able to communicate when you were ready." He motions to a box, but what catches my attention are the iridescent flowers lying unbundled next to it. Why is he giving me something so beautiful? My confusion must show, because he blushes. A thrill shoots through me. I made a demon blush.

"I, uh, picked those for you. I want to apologize for how I've behaved, Zhenechka. I'm so sorry. I've been a bastard to you, and you didn't deserve any of it." His voice wobbles for a second, showing how genuinely broken up about it he really is. I watch him carefully, looking for any sign that he's unstable or playing a game. People rarely say what they mean, or so I've learned. I do not subscribe to the same practice, so I carefully weigh my words before I speak them. My silence must put him on edge, because he continues to talk. "I, uh, picked them in Hell. I don't think they're like anything you have up here, but I thought you might like them."

I take them in, unable to hold back my smile. I cross the small distance to where they lay on the steps and scoop them up. I've never received flowers before, and I'm almost giddy that they've come from my mate. They're fascinating to look at; the patterns definitely reflect their otherworldly origin.

"There's also a phone and something else in the box . . . I programmed my number in there. Astaroth's, too, in case you didn't want to speak to me." His eyes shutter like he's trying to protect himself.

"Thank you. You didn't have to do that, but I appreciate it. I've never gotten flowers before. I'm glad they came from you." He looks surprised. Did he expect me to yell at him for being thoughtful?

His eyes soften. "Thank you for accepting them. I don't want to take up much of your time; I was just trying to drop them off."

"Well, thank you. Again, I appreciate it." I don't know what else there is to say. Maybe I could give him a chance like Astaroth suggested. Actually his words were "I love that demon as if he were my own, but he's an idiot when it comes to emotions. Give him a chance to catch up and adapt, and you'll never find a more loyal man."

"Did you want to come in? I've been able to scrounge together some furniture for the main areas. They had extra chairs and a trunk in the attic. Cheap, but they serve their purpose for now." I gesture for him to walk ahead of me.

I enjoy the unfettered view of his assets as he passes by and makes the journey through the house. So firm. What's the saying? I could bounce a quarter off those babies. He can probably feel my stare, but he'll have to deal. He's delicious. An asshole of epic proportions, apparently, but still delicious. All blond hair and boy next door paired with a wicked smile and those piercing blue eyes. A shiver of arousal goes through me. I've dreamed of how our mating should have gone, wishing we could have started over or met differently. I shake it off. It does me no good to obsess with hypotheticals.

We turn into the dining room turned office, and I take my seat on the worn-out brown faux-leather folding chair I brought down earlier. It leaves the slightly less worn one for Azvameth to sink into. I see the flicker of distaste on his face before he clears it. I pay it no mind. It's obviously not the luxury accommodations he's used to, but it's a giant step up from many places I've been forced to dwell in in the past. A rickety folding chair won't harm my delicate sensibilities.

I turn our attention to his work. "I've gotten a brief idea of what you've been doing. Do you have a plan for tracking Constantine's accomplices? I would like to hear what you know so far."

"You're the authority here, Zhenechka. I know as much as you've shared on the recording." He looks a bit sheepish. Why?

"That's fine. I didn't know if you had extracted any information from the coven members you found and interrogated."

"Um. No, no, they didn't seem to know much."

"Honestly I expect nothing different. Constantine didn't confide in many. As far as resources, do you want to keep this separate from your team?" I must have hit a sore spot, because he flinches.

"Yes. I'd like to let them wrap up what they have going on and do more recon ourselves before involving them."

"Lie." I have no patience for it. I'm not at all a confrontational person, but I won't work with someone who lies to me so easily. I can only tell because I was watching his soul. They darken for a second when someone lies.

"Excuse me?" Anger is present in his voice, but I don't know why.

"I cannot abide by being lied to, even to spare my feelings. I assume that is the reason you won't just say the truth, but it's unnecessary. I'm a big boy; I do not need to be coddled. If you would rather not reveal the reason, I will not force the issue. Just say as much." I keep my voice conversational and light so I don't make him believe I'm accusing him of something. I'm not. "Wanting separation between me and your family makes sense. It's perfectly logical. Any hurt feelings are my own responsibility; I do not blame you for not trusting me around those you care about. Now—"

"That's not why. I mean, it was at first, but I can't merge the two parts of my life without being confident no one will attack you and that it won't affect the team's dynamic."

I process his statement and find no fault. "Fair. When is your next team check-in? Maybe we can reconvene after. I have research I can do from here now that I have access to a phone. We do need to move quickly, but I don't want to rush it and make a mistake."

"We meet weekly unless there's an emergency meeting called. We've had more in the past few weeks than we ever have in such a small amount of time. Would you . . . would you be willing to talk to me this week still?

Even just over the phone? I want to get to know you, Zhen."

I struggle with his request before conceding. "That's fine. I do need you to show me how to work some of it. I've seen them used and talked on them a few times, but I feel very out of my element."

"Shit, yeah, I didn't think about you needing help. I have it set up, but I can show you the main apps." I give him the box back, glancing over at the flowers I placed on the lid of the weathered brown trunk acting like a coffee table.

"Do they require water like normal flowers?"

"Huh? Oh, I think they might. They're grown by our earth and water shadowlings, so I assume they need some sort of water."

"Shadowlings?" I feel my face twitch. I try to keep my fascination out of my voice, but I know I fail.

"Yeah. When low-level demons die again, their soul turns into a shadowling of Hell to supply the realm with power and the elements since they don't exist naturally within it. I have some books from when I was younger that go over most of the workings of Hell. Would you like to borrow them?"

A thrill rushes through me. I love to learn. I can't keep my excitement at bay when I respond. "Absolutely!" I cough and try again. "Yes, please."

He smiles softly at me. "I'll get those for you as soon as I can." The phone he's been fiddling with lights up, and his smile widens. When relaxed, Azvameth is stunning. He adjusts his chair so it's next to mine, leaning into my space to show me the phone. "What all do you need help with?"

I sigh. "I've used a tablet for research, so I understand the mechanics of the internet and some apps. It's the communication part I'm lost on."

He spends a few minutes showing me the call features, including FaceTime. What a wonder. I have always enjoyed the advances in technology from afar. The brilliance of it, how it connects people. I know I could have easily figured it out, but I want to spend a little more time with him. I'm waffling back and forth between needing space and wanting him closer. What kind of space will give him what he needs most?

"Zhen?" I'm torn from my musings.

"Yes?"

"Are you okay? You zoned out there for a while."

"*Da*. I'm fine. Just thinking. I was always prone to drifting mid-conversation when I was younger. I see that special tidbit has come back. I'm sorry; I didn't mean to be rude."

"No apology needed. I can't imagine what coming out of a twenty-year compulsion must feel like. Are you adjusting okay?"

"I think so? I'm, um, not used to doing things because I *want* to do them. It's very unsettling, making decisions." I don't dare make eye contact. I would never hide the truth, but I don't enjoy sharing my vulnerability with him.

"Do you want help with that, Zhen? I-I can help you. I'm here for you. I want us to work. I promised myself if you gave me a chance, I would fight for us. I won't let you down again."

I want to believe Azvameth. His soul shows at least he believes what he's saying. I give him a hesitant nod.

"I'll leave you to think on it. I want you to text me, okay? For anything. Whether it is questions about work or something more personal. I'm hoping for the latter, but I will take what I can get for now." His gaze bores into the side of my face. He leans even further into my space, brushing a soft kiss to my cheek, making it tingle.

My face heats. "I can do that." I sound breathless, which I believe classifies me as "lame," but I'm not sure I can scrounge up enough energy to care one way or another. My shaft thickens at the innocent contact, so I cross my legs to attempt to hide my growing bulge. It has the opposite effect. Az's attention drops to my groin, and his eyes darken. I bite my lip to stifle the whimper clawing its way out. I'm really good with logic. Facts and the scientific process are what make me tick; I've never felt like this before, even when I was a regular mage. My fangs tingle and threaten to lengthen. I need him to go so I can get ahold of myself.

"I think I'm going to turn in. I am having a hard time controlling myself, and I don't like it . . . Well, I don't think I do, anyway. I have very little to compare it to,

83

but I believe my assessment to be true. It's very unsettling."

His eyes widen in humor and a little understanding. "Of course. I did leave you something else in the box; take a look when you're ready. Goodnight, Z." His fingers trace under my eyes, causing them to fall closed. I allow myself to savor the sweet touch of my mate before I reopen them. He steps back and walks through a portal right there in the dining room. Fascinating.

I pick up the box from where he had abandoned it on the floor, catching sight of the old voice recorder. He brought it back? Why?

Chapter Eight

Zhen

I have listened to Azvameth's recording at least a dozen times a day since he left. *Just once more . . . I promise myself,* knowing very well that I told myself that the last three times.

"I'm so sorry, my mate; there is no excuse for what I've done, for what I've said to you. I want to explain what was going through my mind, but it will never justify my actions. I want to know you, but I also want you to know me. The real me—once you strip away my sin and its influence.

I've always admired butterflies. Did you know they don't feel pain? . . ."

The fondness in my mate's voice draws a smile from me. He is so passionate about butterflies, and I find it incredibly endearing. He may have just started feeling rushes of deeper emotions, but I know he's felt at least some of them before. It shows when he's talking about his team and those beautiful winged creatures he's enamored with.

Forgiving Azvameth was easier than I thought it would be. I know I'm holding on to insecurities, but this tape shows me how much he regrets how we met and how he reacted. Sloth demons didn't have mates as far as he knew. He had no idea how to react to what he was seeing, let alone how he was suddenly overcome with feeling. Analyzing the day we met a hundred different ways means I don't see how he could have done anything other than reject me. Could he have listened to my defense? Definitely, but Rhys dying would have sent him into a tailspin anyway. I don't hold it against him. In fact, I was more upset about the following time when he essentially accused me of being a monster, which is rich coming from the man who collects kills like baseball cards.

Listening to the tape, I can see his impulsiveness shining through. He shares so much of himself, holding himself accountable for the shit he's done. He doesn't apologize for his past or anything other than how he reacted to me and how we met. He's unapologetic about liking his job, at being good at it. After a lot of thought, he understands that he hated my actions because they weren't actually mine. He hated that he had no one alive to blame and that he couldn't just kill Constantine over and over again like he wanted to.

It doesn't excuse him, but I do understand him a bit better. Pretty words aren't all I'm going to go by, though. He has to continue to show me in actions; I just have to work up the nerve to contact him first since he promised to give me time.

I roll my eyes as I tuck the recorder in my pocket, continuing to listen as I go about my nightly routine. After I meditate outside, I lock up, though that won't stop anyone with half a mind to get in. My phone mocks me from the counter as I pass through the kitchen to the backyard. I don't have the courage to text Azvameth yet, but I told myself I would do it tomorrow. I even added it to the list!

My strength has increased significantly since I've fed from Astaroth and the bagged blood. It was hard not to gorge myself, but I want to make the blood testing as controlled as possible with day-to-day activities, so I refrain from drinking more than the one bag every other day. The sharp pains of hunger have abated, leaving me . . . not full, exactly, just content. I click the sliding door shut behind me and wander to the patch of yard I've decided will be my meditation area. The area has more grass than sticks, so it doesn't hurt to sit for long periods. I pull the recorder out of my pocket and plop down, arranging myself in a cross-legged position and breathing deep before turning off the recording. I clear my mind, slipping into a relaxed state much faster than I have in days. In, out.

Once I feel properly grounded, I let my mind wander while taking stock of my body. It's harder to find my magic now than it used to be, and I once again lament my inability to explore my ability in the past twenty years. Anger and a dash of frustration at being back at my previous seven-year-old power level are justified but not useful. I push away the emotions as best I can and try not to continue to grieve my loss of elemental magic. I had known in my heart that it was gone when I transformed, but I never had the chance to prove it in a tangible way. Accepting it has been hard, but I try not to dwell.

Done meditating, I stand smoothly, glad my joints don't creak like they would have if I hadn't been made a vampire. I make my way to the well, pumping the rusted handle until cloudy water emerges and splashes into the trusty metal bucket I've been using for everything. I fill the bucket halfway before getting up and lumbering over to tie the rope I used on the deer to the handle to hoist it above the fire pit I made for cooking.

Exhausted from today's events, I almost skip washing up and head to bed, but my self-discipline will not allow it. I despise being dirty. Choosing to stay standing, I attempt to create a small fire with the tiny bits of flint I have left. I've been rationing it to boil the water for eating, but the idea of using cold well water to wash makes my lip curl. Like a clumsy asshole, I drop the rest of the flint into the flame, and the fire roars to life at least triple the size I was going for. Flames lick the sides of the bucket, precariously close to the rope. I try to pull the rope back, but the whole situation gets away from me. I have to rely on the water by pushing some from the bucket, splashing the flames into submission. I severely misjudged the angle and almost all of the water sloshes out of the bucket, dousing the fire completely. Fuck! Now I have no clean water, no fire to boil more, and my flint is gone. I throw my hands in the air and let out my frustration.

"Son of a—mother fu—shit bucket—no good—goddamned—DONKEY!" My bellowing could probably be heard for miles, but I can't bring myself to care. I'm dirty and tired and at the end of my rope. I leave the mess as is and stomp back into the rickety farmhouse, beelining it straight to my phone. I pick it up and pull up the messaging app and start a text to Azvameth before I can talk myself out of it.

Me: *I can't do this.*

I hit send before I think of the fact that he will probably respond. Instead of the dots indicating that he's typing, the phone rings in my hand, making me freeze. My anger swiftly drains from me, replaced with panic. After a bit, the ringing stops, and a text pops up before I can decide what to do about the missed call.

Azvameth: *Please, Zhen.*

Confused, I re-read my message and blanch. He obviously has no context, so I won't blame him for jumping to the worst-case scenario. Ugh, now I have to call him back. I take a deep breath and click the few icons to bring me to his contact and hit the phone symbol, exhaling heavily.

He answers before the first ring completes. "Zhenechka? Are you okay?" His worry soothes the harsh edges of my discomfort.

"Ummm, fine, yes. I'm fine." Why can't I respond like a normal person?

"Oh. I'm sorry, I hate pushing, but I need to know, what can't you do? If it's me or if I crossed a line with the recording—"

"No! No. It's not you. Honestly I was just having a bad night trying to get warm water for washing, and my new routine was disturbed, which apparently makes me incredibly cranky. I'm sorry for worrying you."

"You don't have hot water?! Why didn't you say something?"

I let the silence extend, not knowing how to respond without sounding like I'm trying to open old wounds. It's not like I had a way to contact him, or a chance to tell him the day of the rejection. I settle for the least confrontational option, yet it's still one hundred percent true. "Umm, the only water is pumped from the well out back. There is no running water here currently. Maybe a pipe burst back in the day since there's no real reason for it not to work. I'm not sure, though. I'm not very handy."

"Fuck. I'm sorry, Zhen. I should have checked the house out more before leaving you there. I have a solution, but if you don't want to do it, there's no pressure. I have a hotel room with tons of hot water. I can portal you here so you can relax in a hot shower or bath, and then when you're ready to go home, I can bring you back . . . or you can stay with me here until I can arrange a team to renovate the farmhouse to make it livable."

"You don't have to do all that, but I would appreciate a shower. I haven't had a real shower in years." I feel close to tears just thinking of being truly clean.

"Let me put pants on and I'll come right to you. Dining room, okay?" I hear rustling like he's rummaging for said pants.

"*Da*. I'll grab a change of clothes from the previous owners here and be down as soon as I can. Is it safe for me to go with you through the portal? I'm not completely sure how that all works." My nervousness must be audible, because he chuckles softly.

"It's safe, Z. I wouldn't suggest bringing more than a person or two at a time, but you won't be a problem or strain at all. I gathered some reading material for you like we talked about. One of them covers portals, if that helps?"

I blush, thankful he's not here to witness it. "Yes, th-thank you."

"All right . . . See you in a few." The phone disconnects, and seconds later I hear his heartbeat downstairs.

The dining room is dark but not pitch black. A lone lantern near the hall gives minimal light to the rooms surrounding it. As I cross the room, I wonder idly if Zhen's night vision is the same as a regular vampire's or if the light is there by necessity.

I hear his movements upstairs as he shuffles around the blue room and then heads toward the stairs. He emerges from the hall into the landing overlooking the foyer, holding a bundle of clothing against his chest and his new phone in his hand. I give him a soft smile when our gazes connect, trying to reassure him. The tightness around his eyes shows his stress, but he tries to cover it with a smile in return. I'd love it if he never came back here until we figured out if and when we could redo the place, but his attachment seems, understandably, pretty solid.

Once he takes the last step off the old stairs, I am pulled toward him as if we were magnets. His broad shoulders are drawn in slightly as if he's trying to hide his size, but his steps are sure. My mate is full of such contradictions. I haven't been bored in his presence once, which is crazy in itself. I can't remember anything other than butterflies keeping my attention so long, but with him I could lose myself for hours just staring at those sage eyes.

"Do you have everything you need? I can wait for you to grab a bag if you have one?"

"*Da.* This is it. I grabbed some clothes that looked like they might fit. I'll admit I've never worn coveralls before, so I don't know how aesthetically pleasing it will be, but I do not have much of a choice."

I chuckle, trying to imagine my nerdy mate in a farmer getup. "If it doesn't work out, I have plenty of clothes you can have. I'm not the best judge of fashion, but all my clothes have been Kieran approved." At his questioning eyebrow lift, I hasten to explain. "Kieran does all my shopping for me. He's the lust demon on my team. I would wear the same outfit every day—I don't care much what I'm dressed in, more on how well it disguises the inevitable bloodstains. He and Kek take that as an insult to fashion, I guess." I shrug.

He grins. "I might just take you up on the offer of clothes. I don't think these will be too comfortable." He sets the bundle down and rummages in the pile for a second, pulling out the recorder and quickly shoving it into his front pants pocket with a blush like if he were fast enough, I wouldn't be able to see anything. His embarrassed, flushed face makes my dick perk up and demand attention. I suppress a groan, trying to hide my arousal.

His head tilts to the side, brow furrowed. "Are you okay? Your heart rate increased, and you look like you're in pain. Are you hurt?" Jesus, this guy is adorable.

"Ah, no. Not hurt. Just trying to behave. I don't want to make you uncomfortable."

"Why would I—oh! Oh. Oooooohhhhhh. So you're—?" He motions to the pretty obvious tent in my pants.

I can't hold back my shock of laughter. "Yeah, I'm—" I motion to my bulge. He blushes again and ducks his chin, but not before I catch his small smile. I take pity on my mate and change the subject. "Are you ready for that hot shower I promised?" He nods quickly and rushes to stand in front of me, head still tilted down. I open a portal to my right and hold my elbow out for him to take. "Shall we?"

We walk through the portal, stepping into the living area I've come to see as a second home in the past few days, more than just the hookup pad it started out as. I usher him toward the bathroom, not rushing him per se, but now that my mate is here, there are definitely a few things I need to fix before he gets the wrong idea . . . like the condom wrappers I never picked up off the floor next to the bed from the tryst with the wolf-and-demon couple. I hadn't had the cleaners in because I wasn't planning on hooking up with anyone, so the lingering scents never bothered me, but I don't know if my mate will see it the same way.

"Are you all right, Azvameth?" Zhen's question yanks me from my thoughts. His light eyes hold no censure, only curiosity and concern.

"Yes. I'm sorry. I was thinking about what you could wear and be comfortable." His face falls and I flinch. Right. Lie detector. "Okay, uh . . . truth? I'm panicking because you're here with me finally and I never anticipated it happening without the cleaners coming in, so I'm trying to remember everything that could upset you so I can get rid of it before you're done with your shower." I grimace. There was definitely a more tactful way of saying all that, but he just looks softly at me.

"I don't expect you to not have had a few partners before you met me, Az. Would it have been nice not to smell them all over your bedroom? Yes. But the scents are old, and I won't hold it against you. Thank you for being honest with me."

I blow out a heavy sigh. I lucked out on my mate being so understanding, for sure. "I have some clothes I can grab if you want to jump in the shower. Feel free to use as much hot water as you want. I can just set the clothes on the counter?" He chews his lip a bit and then nods.

"Oh! Did you eat tonight? I mean, drink? I don't know how you'd rather me ask." God, I'm so fucking awkward.

His smooth chuckle washes over me. "I'm fine for tonight, Azvameth. To answer your question, I'm used to calling it 'feed' since I can also eat and drink regular items." His eyes crinkle as he smiles broadly.

Zhen must decide to take pity on me and heads to the bathroom, leaving the door cracked. I stand frozen, staring at the sliver of open doorway like it holds the answers to the universe. It just might if it means I get to see my mate naked. I can't see anything from this angle, but I can hear the fabric of his clothes running along his body as he strips. Is Zhen imagining me watching him?

I'm knocked from my musing by the water starting. I head to the dresser and rifle through the second drawer that houses the stretchy sweats the whole team prefers on casual days so we can switch between forms without ruining clothes. Picking a plain black tee and grey sweatpants, I head to the bathroom to place them on the counter.

Am I aware I never chose underwear for him to wear? Absolutely. Seeing his body encased in grey sweatpants and watching his dick bounce with each step is not something I'm willing to pass up.

Thick air and steam greet me as I tap the door all the way open and step into the bathroom. Unfortunately this hotel has an opaque white shower curtain, so I can't see Zhen, but my imagination is running wild with images of water sluicing down his chest and back. I set the clothes on the counter and take a step toward the shower, clearing my throat, trying to force words from my mouth until I hear a hiccup in his breathing. I can't tell if he's trying not to cry or if it's from arousal, but I need to make sure he's okay. "Zhen?"

Another hiccup. "Yes, Azvameth?" Definitely emotion and not all hot and bothered. My dick deflates like a balloon.

"Are you okay?" I take another tentative step toward the shower. I'm close enough I can run my fingers along the curtain if I just reach out.

"Yes? I mean, yes. I'm fine . . . almost done. Would you mind waiting? Uh, in the other room?"

"Of course. Holler if you need anything." I spin toward the door, my chest aching at my mate trying to be strong and not sharing his stress with me. I want to comfort him but haven't the faintest clue how. I pace, using the area between the couch and the bedroom door, listening to him turn off the water and towel dry. I know when he notices the lack of undergarments because he lets out a squeak, and I can't help my snicker.

The door swings open, and a damp Zhen strolls out, showing no evidence of his earlier upset. I carefully watch his face for signs of distress, but I find none. "I know you just came for the shower, but did you want to stay a little longer? I can order room service, and we could watch a movie? No funny business. I just . . ." I let my words trail off, not sure how to finish that sentence. *I just need to be close to you because my chest hurts all the time and I can't stop thinking about you and I've never felt like this before and I want to crawl inside of you and keep you safe.* Yeah, no. He'll think I'm nuts.

Unaware of my creepy-ass thoughts, he utters a soft, "Yeah, Az, I can do that," as his shoulders slump in relief.

Zhen

We're settled on the couch in front of the TV, bodies not quite touching. I haven't paid the least bit of attention to the movie playing, too focused on his human-like body next to mine and the tension thrumming between us. He can't sit still, constantly fidgeting beside me. Maybe he's bored and just doesn't know how to ask me to leave?

97

"Do you want me to go?" I hope my insecurities aren't plastered all over my face, but when he whips his head to the left to look at me, I know I failed.

"No!" He clears his throat. "I really don't want you to leave."

His heartbeat has been up and down since we sat down, so I'm not surprised that it's racing again. He's not lying; he does want me here. So why is he so awkward? Normally that's my thing. "Is everything okay, then? You just seem a little all over the place, and I don't understand." He chokes on nothing, making my eyes widen.

"I'm trying to be good, Zhen. I really want to throw you down in front of the couch and rub all over you like an animal in heat. We just started talking for real, and I *really* don't want to scare you off, but I have to stop myself from reaching for you every two fucking seconds."

Wow, okay. I know I'm blushing, and he groans in response, making my face heat even more.

"That's . . . I'm . . ." Words. I need words, but they evade me. Would he feel the same way knowing I'm so inexperienced I'd probably come in my pants the second he threw me around? I close my eyes and take a deep breath. "We need to do words—I mean, talk. Yes, talk, that's the thing we should do."

A low rumble sounds from him, and I pop my eyes open to see his face hard and eyes heated. "That pretty flush is not really making it better." He reaches down and adjusts himself.

"I-I don't. I don't know how to respond to that. I've never had anyone say something like that to me before. Do I say thank you? I'm unaware of the . . . social etiquette surrounding arousal." There. Words.

"Never? I can't believe that. Wait. So you've never had anyone *tell* you they want to fuck you, but you've like . . ." He trails off, jaw open, like the idea that I'm a virgin broke his brain.

"Is it bad? That I'm a virgin? I know you're experienced, like really experienced if your heart rate is anything to go by. I know you were probably looking forward to having an experienced mate to fulfill your needs. I heard a joke once about sloth demons and their want for extreme sex. I have no frame of reference as far as what would be extreme or not, but judging by the tone of the individual who told the joke, I assume someone just trying to figure out if they're a top or a bottom would be displeasing. I—"

I didn't realize how much I had been rambling until he cut me off with the press of his soft lips to mine. Tingles shoot through my body, and my hand reflexively grasps his shoulder to ground me. His tongue swipes over my bottom lip, and I gasp. Az takes full advantage, invading my mouth with his tongue and pressing his chest to mine. I melt into the firm touch, letting him take control, and am rewarded with a deep moan. He pulls back, and I whimper, causing him to press a few more chaste but sensual pecks onto my swollen lips before pulling away completely.

"You have no idea how badly I need you exactly as you are. I hate that I damaged us so badly. I'm so sorry, mate. Even if making out like younglings is all we ever do, I would be more than satisfied. My devotion to you is not conditional, Zhen, and I know you cannot trust it yet . . . but I *will* earn it." He runs a hand soothingly up and down my arm as his eyes implore me to believe him. "Stay with me tonight?"

His soul reaches for mine again, like it did that first day, and this time I revel in it. His soul is glowing, desperate for our bond, and I take the chance knowing full well that if he rejects me again, I may not survive. "Okay, Az. I'll stay."

Chapter Nine

Azvameth

I wake up to an arm draped over my chest and soft puffs of warm air on my neck. I don't want to wake Zhen; we were up really late talking. I got to hear more about his family, and I told him all about my team. I was finally able to give him the books I'd been hoarding for him, and remembering the look of reverence he gave them warms me. My bladder protests my lack of hustle, but I can spare a few minutes. Rolling over so I face my mate jostles him a bit, and his eyes fly open in a panic, muscles bunching like he's ready to fight me. I watch as recognition dawns and a sweet smile transforms his beautiful face.

"Good morning, mate." I lean in to give him a quick kiss but am distracted by the plushness of his lips. Unable to resist a taste, I slip his lower lip between mine and pull, requesting access. He readily complies, giving himself over to me completely. His hips twitch toward me as I gently suck on his tongue, the feel of his erection against mine making my head spin. I pull back enough to slide my mouth over his jaw and down his neck. Zhen bares his throat and makes delightful little sounds as I suck a beautiful bruise to life where his shoulder meets his neck. I chuckle and continue my way down to his chest as he pants heavily with the pain. His pale nipples call to me, and I can't resist nibbling on them as he strains against me. We took our shirts off before bed to stay comfortable. So smart.

"Please, Az. *Plez*. More." Listening to him slip in a Russian "please" sets my blood on fire. I follow his command for more and bite harder, rewarded by a flinch followed by a desperate moan before he presses his chest into me, seeking more pleasure-pain. I slide a hand up his neck and wrap it around his throat gently, watching for his reaction. His light-green eyes flash with need, so I squeeze my hand a little harder before letting go. I skim my fingers down to where waistband meets skin, following with my mouth and sucking more marks as I go. I flick my gaze to meet his and tug on his sweats, asking for permission to lower them. He whimpers again and nods, looking both nervous and excited. I pull them down until they slip from his legs completely. My mouth waters as I take in the sight of his sinful body as a whole before turning my attention to the apex of his thighs.

"Beautiful," I murmur.

His uncut cock lies hard and heavy against his happy trail, the pink head peeking out. I cannot resist the invitation and nip at his foreskin, dipping my tongue inside to tease the underside of his head. His breathless squeal sounds above me in warning. I can tell my mate is close, so I stretch my arm back up to grip his throat, cutting off his oxygen as I swallow his shaft down to the hilt. He grabs my wrist and I lighten up immediately, watching under my lashes as he gulps in breaths and arches back, his bottom half completely leaving the bed as his spend pulses down my throat. Moaning, I continue to swallow around his length until he flinches away, oversensitive. His hand stays around my wrist, slowly pulling my palm up to his mouth, and he kisses my palm as I gently lick him clean.

A phone ringing causes me to pause my *very* thorough cleaning of Zhen's beautiful body. The ringtone is not mine, so I know automatically that it's Astaroth. My mate seems to be out of it still, so I reach over to the phone I'd put on the charger for him last night on the nightstand. A glance at the screen confirms my suspicion.

"This better be important, dear duke." I know I'm being snarky, but I wanted to bask in the afterglow with my mate, not have my aching balls shrivel up into my body as I talk to my boss. Why would he be calling Zhen, anyway?

"Hello, Azvameth. I assume Zhenechka is with you?" I glance down and catch the humor and curiosity in Zhen's gaze as he holds out his hand. I don't respond to Astaroth before huffing and handing the phone over and cuddling up to Zhen's side, resting my head on his chest. Snuggling is definitely not something I've done before. Usually I can't get rid of my companions fast enough, but with my mate I want to become a fucking barnacle apparently. He greets my boss as he wraps his arm around me, shuffling to get us both comfortable. Some small talk ensues before my Zhen cuts to the chase, making me smile.

"What can I do for you, sir?" Zhen asks.

I can hear Astaroth's humor as he responds. "I am actually following up on your requests. I dropped the medical supplies off at the farmhouse. I was surprised to not find you there, so I thought I would call and give you an update instead of barging into the hotel room Azvameth doesn't think I know about." He's grinning through the phone, I can tell. Smug bastard.

"Oh! Thank you so much. I'm excited to get back to my research. You said requests, like plural. Does that mean you also found a way or time to have me meet with the rescued souls? I know you said you trust me around them, but are you sure?"

"Absolutely, Zhen. I know a few have mentioned you, asking about your welfare. Rhys especially." Zhen glows while he thanks Astaroth and sets up a time next week for him to go to the safe house. I agree to take him via portal and accompany him while he makes his rounds.

First, though, I need to talk to Aridam. The impending conversation I have to have with the wrath demon makes me less nervous, but I'm not quite ready for my worlds to collide. I want to be in a better place with my mate before throwing him into the fire that is my team. I also worry about how he will react to the other demons' sins. Since he's not human, I don't believe it'll be terrible, but I'm still cautious.

I set up the meeting for an hour later, knowing Aridam will be available. I need to explain what's been going on, and I know my team has been worried about me, especially Bel and Rhys, but the only one I answer to is Ari, so he will be the only one I explain myself to. I have no idea how this is going to go, though. My phone buzzes again, so I pull it out of my shorts pocket to check.

Aridam: *Don't keep me waiting, Az.*

I snort and type back a quick reply before portaling to the dining room we've made our temporary base until Ari's team house is built. I vaguely wonder if I will be residing there with everyone or if I'll be at the awful farmhouse Zhen currently occupies.

Aridam is lounging in his chair like he hasn't a care in the world. I can see his act for what it is, though. I wouldn't have noticed, or cared to notice, before Zhen . . . but now I'm actually acquainted with the abhorrent way my chest constricts and sometimes I can't breathe correctly. Worry. Ick. At least Aridam won't bring it up so we can both pretend icky feelings aren't happening. Yes, pretending is a good plan. Wonderful, even.

I find a seat at the table and slide in. I picked one not too close to be within swiping distance but not far enough away to be disrespectful. I do, however, keep myself between the wrath demon and the door. I don't expect him to attack me, not really, but I refuse to be a sitting duck if I'm wrong. Once I'm settled in the chair and there's enough silence for Ari to feel me tense, he speaks.

"So what is it? What is so important, Azvameth?" I flinch at the genuine confusion and the little bit of hurt I hear in his voice.

"There was a situation. I-I couldn't be there, Aridam. I couldn't leave him."

"Explain. Nothing could have kept me from supporting you if our roles had been reversed. Nothing except maybe Rhys. So you tell me why someone I called a friend wasn't there for me or for Rhys of all people. I thought you liked him?"

"What?! I do! Of course I do, mostly. I just couldn't face you because he's my mate!" A low growl sounds from deep within his chest, and his eyes start to swirl. I rush to correct his line of thought. "Not Rhys. Zhenechka. You know him as Ivan. He's my mate. How could I face you knowing it's because of my mate that yours carries the scars he does?"

Aridam's face freezes as he tries to process the information I've dumped all over him. His eyes flit back and forth between regular grey and swirling silver, showing Wrath is trying to fight for control. I know it could take a while for him to gain the upper hand, so I wait with bated breath to see if he's going to kick my ass right now or wait until later.

Ari's eyes settle, and I let out a breath. Thankfully it looks like I'll get a pass. "You know I hate this as much as you do, right?" He looks doubtful. I try again. "I hate knowing my mate was under that psychopath's compulsion for so long. I hate that I reacted without thinking things through or waiting for answers and crushed him with my angry, impulsive outburst, and I hate that the damage might be irreparable. I feel helpless, Aridam."

Understanding softens his gaze. "Mates throw your world into chaos, Azvameth. It's a good thing. I don't know what I would do without Rhys." Pain hangs heavily in the air, and I assume he's working through flashbacks of his mate's death. He shakes his head, like he's physically dislodging the memories from the front of his mind.

"He saved Rhys at that farmhouse more than once. Your mate is special, Azvameth. I don't need to know details right now, but Rhys will be excited to know he's okay. He was worried after he woke up that Ivan, uh, Zhenechka was in danger."

"No! You can't tell him yet. I need more time." My voice rises higher than I intend, belying my panic. "It's nothing against the team, not anymore, but I want to be on more solid ground with Zhen before I throw him into the team's dynamic. He's innocent in a lot of things but brilliant in others. I know he'll be fine, but I want him to be able to go at his own pace."

Aridam's scowl doesn't lift when he replies, "I will not lie to my mate. I won't volunteer the information you've shared, other than we spoke, but if he asks about things specifically? I will tell him, and I won't feel an ounce of remorse."

"Understood. Thank you." I just stand there awkwardly, not knowing how to end the conversation. Ugh, feelings are weird. Normally I would just leave and not think twice; it was so much easier.

"Leave, Azvameth. It seems we both have mates to attend to," he says roughly as he stands, leaving the conference room before I do at a pace quicker than I really expected of him. I want to laugh at his eagerness to get back to Rhys, but I completely understand his rush.

Opening a portal directly into the hotel bedroom, I'm treated to the sight of my mate in just a towel and still dripping wet. I groan as I step in, making him spin toward me and almost drop his small covering.

"You're back! I had a thought about what we should do today, and I *really* want to go to the farmhouse to check out the new supplies. Will you take me? You don't have to stay if it's boring . . ."

He looks like he's talking himself out of my company, and I can't have that, so I interrupt quickly. "Of course I'll stay with you while we're there, Zhen. I wanted to take a look at the surrounding land anyway. I can do that once you start doing your science-y stuff. Sound good?"

He nods vehemently and doesn't ask why I would want to look at the land. I watch as he rushes to dress after pulling out another set of my clothes. He only flashes his tight pale ass at me for a second, but it's enough for blood to rush south, making me painfully hard. *His pace.* The reminder lifts the fog of lust just a smidge, trying to let my head run things. Less fun than letting my dick run things, but more worthwhile.

Maybe I could bloody something to distract myself to be good.

I swiftly pack a bag, not checking my clothing since they're all the same. I throw in extra, knowing my mate doesn't have much. For Zhen, I pick the more colorful items from the back of my closet that I've acquired but never actually worn. Color seems more his speed, but he can take whatever he wants out of my suitcase when we get to the old, dilapidated farmhouse.

After throwing in my basic toiletries, I'm finished and my duffle is close to bursting. I can hear movement in the kitchenette, so I head that way. Holding the complimentary pad of paper the hotel gives and the matching maroon pen, Zhen is hunched over and scribbling like a madman. I have no idea what his brilliant mind has done, but I can feel his excitement.

I simply watch, knowing he is aware of my presence, but I don't want to disturb his train of thought by speaking. His concentration is adorable; the small amount of tongue that peeks between his lips as he scrunches his nose is endearing as fuck. My little scientist.

His head pops up when he's done scribbling, and his excitement shows through his wide smile. "I have a theory about blood potency! I just need a few vials from different species of supes again so I can test it correctly for my own purposes." His smile fades a bit. "All the research was lost, which I understand completely; I just don't know how to accomplish gathering all of it again. I don't want to hurt anyone." He frowns hard before looking excited again.

"There is a difference, though, between blood given versus blood taken forcefully, did you know? I hadn't experienced it until Astaroth. I want to see how different the energy is when the soul is not in distress. The possibilities are fascinating, don't you think?"

Gah, even his ramble is adorable. This hulking vampire hybrid is so oblivious and sweet I can't stand it. "It sounds as if you have quite the plan, my mate. I bet you will have more willing donors than you think if you want me to talk to my team once we're more settled. Astaroth and his minions too, of course."

I hate even mentioning the duke to him. I know my mate has no romantic feelings for my boss, but my jealousy doesn't seem to care. The intensity of general feelings is becoming easier to handle, but once Zhen is physically next to someone, I don't have much faith in my control if someone were to flirt with or touch him. My fingers start to itch just thinking about it, like my claws will pop out at any time.

"Do you think so?" His smile is back to full brightness, and my heart tugs at his awe over someone caring. It makes me want to spoil the shit out of him.

Shaking my head with a put-upon sigh, I pick up the notebook he has been using and then hold out my arm like a real fucking gentleman. He takes my arm and presses into me a little as I open a portal and walk him through. I take a look around the farmhouse with a critical eye as he immediately goes in search of the supplies our dear duke dropped off for him.

We have a choice. We can keep the farmhouse and redo it to fit us or find somewhere else. I'm not thrilled by the thought of keeping the house Rhys died in or where my mate was forced to torture himself and others. He wanted to stay, though, so I should wait and see why he wanted to stay in the first place.

If we stay, the renovation is going to be extensive. I had an inkling before, but the list grows ever longer as I go from room to room. Even though we hopefully won't stay, the work needs done if we want to sell it or give it to a beta team. Maybe I should run it by the boss. I pull out my phone and call Franco, knowing he'll know which team needs another house up here just in case and who to put me in touch with to get reno done quickly and quietly.

"Yes, Azvameth? I'm a little busy coordinating your entire team's move to a new house up there. What could you possibly need from me right now?" His tone is biting, which throws me off. I've never heard Franco frazzled.

"I don't know what crawled up your ass, but you should have someone look into it. Sounds painful, to be honest. Not my kink, but whatever floats your boat." My droll tone is on point.

"I hate you. What do you want?" His voice sounds less dangerous after my comment, so I feel more confident asking him.

"I need a team to overhaul Zhen's farmhouse. It's shit and I can't stand it. It doesn't even have running water or electricity, Franco. Honestly I would love to just hand the house over to you guys to deal with, but I need to run it by Zhen. Also, don't hate me, but do you know of another place kind of near the new team house for sale in case he's willing to leave?"

"Well, damn. Okay, I can see the problem. There is one property, but it's as big of a problem as the house you're in right now. For either job I would suggest Hamish and his team, but they're working with Aridam right now. Hmmm, how about Dane? He was a part of the pack Alpha Gregory deserted and left to fend for themselves. He's got a crew, I think, but he still visits the other souls at the safe house pretty regularly. I'd give you his contact info, but I can't do that with any of the damaged or rescued souls. Let me talk to Astaroth and see what we can do."

"That works. I'll send over my mate's decision the second he makes one." I want to be done talking now, so I just hang up. He's used to it; he'll be fine. Zhen's chiding voice in my head makes me send a quick *I hope your day gets better* text to soften the blow. Gross. I gag and shake off the weird feelings and hunt down my mate.

Chapter Ten

Zhen

Bzzt. Bzzt. The vibrations of incoming texts sound against the counter from the other room. I smile to myself, knowing it's only one of two people calling, and since my mate is wandering around here somewhere, I know it's Astaroth. I want to rush to finish my notes, but I won't compromise the tests I'm currently running. He was kind enough to send over medical supplies like I asked—top-of-the-line items that are so much easier to work with without help—so I feel confident he won't mind waiting for a reply from me.

Making sure to jot down the cells' behavior as thoroughly as possible, I finally finish and pack up the equipment. Normally I would leave it out after cleaning, but Azvameth and I are leaving soon, and I don't want anything to happen to the expensive supplies I've been gifted while we're gone.

The hall closet has since been cleared out and acts as supply storage for now. The old farmhouse has become a bit more comfortable in the past few days, battery-operated lights and some extra desk space being the biggest changes. We can't do any renovations here or at the new place until we meet with Dane, and since that's not happening until later today, we've just been splitting our time between the farmhouse and the hotel room.

Azvameth finally came to me about our living situations, and we quickly realized we are both idiots and need to communicate better. Neither of us had wanted to rock the boat, so we were contemplating staying here even though neither of us wanted it—the opposite, in fact. I would be happy never to step foot here again. Once it's fixed we will hand it over to Astaroth and he'll do whatever he wants with it.

Azvameth's inability to sit still hasn't improved, meaning he's been popping up all over the place while I work. When we settle in for the night at the hotel, he seems calmer and engaged, not showing any impatience at my need to talk everything out. I've gotten to know some of his quirks, and they mesh perfectly with mine so far, which is a huge weight off my shoulders. I want this to work; I'm just a bit of a "chicken shit," like my older brother used to taunt.

I'm incredibly curious, though, at what certain bedroom activities Azvameth wants to try. I catch him zoning enough to know he's got quite the list for us, but he's not making a move. The kid gloves will come off eventually, hopefully. I had wanted to go slow, but the glacial pace he's set is driving me crazy.

I startle when Az's voice sounds from behind me. "Is there something particularly interesting about the closet? You've been staring at the contents for a while."

"Oh, hush, I was thinking. What time are we leaving?" Shit, I forgot. I need to check my messages. I half listen for Azvameth's answer as I rush to my phone, only to find random numbers with no context in a text.

"We are just waiting for our duke to send the coordinates and give us the all clear."

"Oh! That's what these are. Perfect, here. I have my bag ready by the door. Do we need to lock up?"

"Nope, Lily will be popping by any minute to put up the wards. Do you want to wait and meet her or just head out?" His tone suggests he isn't the fondest of the witch, though he's not really fond of anyone, save me, so I can't judge a person outside of the team by whether my sloth demon approves.

"Can we stay? I want to watch her process and meet her since she'll be doing our new place too. She is pretty close to some of your team, you said? We should make an effort to be nice, right?" He simply grunts in return, probably not liking the idea of being nice to a person for no reason. So prickly. "It will only be a few minutes, *babochka*. You can fake it for a few minutes, right?" I've never given anyone their own nickname before, but calling him butterfly makes his face heat, and his shy smile warms me.

"Knock knock!" A feminine voice carries into the house. An extra heartbeat has me curious. Of course, she would need someone to pop her over here, but I wonder who it is and if they're from Az's team.

The opening door reveals a curvy little brunette woman with a sophisticated air about her. Elegant, almost. I peek at her soul and am struck with how wonderful she is as a person. I want to befriend this little witch.

She must get sick of my silent staring because she thrusts her hand in front of her. "Lily Stronghold, pleasure to meet you. I've heard a few things about you, but nothing that makes sense."

"Ah, well, sorry about that. It's been quite the circus. I'm Zhenechka Morozov."

"Wait. Zhenechka. Morozov. Like *the* Zhenechka Morozov? Part of the most mysterious and prestigious coven in history?"

I cough awkwardly at her assessment. "Umm, yes? We were mages, though, if that explains anything."

"Oh, I knew you weren't regular magic users. Some covens already knew but never told the secret. Your family protected so many of us. I'm so sorry for your loss."

I feel the back of my eyes tingling, so I simply nod and look away. I catch sight of the demon who brought her. Stunning, so much so that I suck in a sharp breath. This must be Kieran. I'm not so close that I'm influenced by lust, but that doesn't stop me from recognizing how beautiful he is. He's quietly chatting with Az, leaning in to whisper, like that will do anything but hide his words from Lily. I can hear every word now that I'm paying attention.

". . . his scars are permanent. Lily hasn't been able to find anyone strong enough with enough knowledge to alter his scarring."

Rhys. I know that's who they're talking about. I take a deep breath and focus back on Lily, who is watching me with a mixture of curiosity and excitement.

"I heard that today you're meeting the souls they rescued. Are you excited? You're a soul mage, right? That's what Kieran implied before we got here. Do you think you can help them?"

She pulls no punches, does she? "I'm not sure. I need to examine them first. Each one suffered differently, and there is only so much I can do. It's not like I can just magically fix them."

Her eyebrows rise in surprise. "Oh. Okay. Admittedly, I don't know much about soul mages and how the abilities work, so I'll take your word for it. Anyway, let's get this place warded! If you could just hold this for a minute." She shoves a clear crystal into my hand and calls for Azvameth to do the same, tossing his over to where he is still talking to the other demon. He snatches it from the air without pausing his conversation or looking away. Refocusing, I raise an eyebrow at the witch's assumption that Az will get full entry, but she just winks and nods. What does that mean?

I shake my head and just wait for her to deem me done. "Perfect! I'll be able to use these to push your energy signature into the wards so it responds to you two and only you. There's enough crazy in this world that I don't want to extend the wards to more people quite yet. Mine are connected to me, so I can give permissions as I see fit, but not being a witch is hampering your ward style, my friend."

Ahh, so that's how it works. Fascinating.

Azvameth wanders back over with his crystal, eyes sweeping over me with enough heat that I start to sweat a little. Damn demon.

"Hey, Lily, we have to get going. Do you need anything else from us, or are we good to go?" He's impatient now, shifting from foot to foot.

"Oh! Yeah, you guys are good. Go ahead and set the quartz right here." She unrolls a soft cloth and gestures for us to plop them on it. My mate follows her directions without asking questions, so I assume it's just a witch thing and let it go.

"Ready?" he asks me softly, holding out his arm for me to hold. I nod and follow his lead through the portal. As we step through, he groans.

"What? What happened?" I thought portals didn't hurt him.

"Get ready, Z. You're about to meet some of my team." He huffs a frustrated breath, letting go of my arm and almost trudging toward the house.

"Should I be worried?" I follow a short distance behind him, nervous that he disconnected from me because he's still ashamed to be fated to me. He spins at my tone and grabs my hand, dragging me to him. My chest gently bumps his, his mouth finding mine. His kiss obliterates my doubts, clears my mind of all thoughts, actually. He deepens it, tongue pushing into my mouth until I whimper with need. My wanton noises must remind him that we aren't really alone, because he slowly pulls back, pressing a soft kiss to my nose before whispering reassurances that everything will be fine.

I don't have time to formulate a response before a voice calls out, "Hey! Stop sucking face! You're hogging him. Rude, man."

Azvameth snarls in response, but I can hear the lack of any real malice. I spy Rhys standing on the porch, leaning over the freshly painted banister with both hands braced on the wood. I don't see his mate, but I assume he's nearby. I tense, looking around as covertly as I can. I fail miserably, of course, because Rhys snorts out a laugh. "He's inside. Don't worry, I don't think the big guy will come after you. I mean, probably not. Maybe." He looks less confident now. "Eh, just stay next to Az so he can get ya out if Wrath decides to throw a tantrum, yeah?"

I nod quickly as Az chuckles. "Come on, it'll be fine." We walk the rest of the distance to the house. We don't make it to the bottom of the stairs before I'm tackled into a hug by the human.

"Thank you, Zhenechka. I don't want to dwell on everything or it'll give me some crazy nightmares and that's icky, but thank you. I know you did everything you could."

"How? How did you know? I didn't say a single word to you." My voice trembles, so he squeezes me harder.

"I just knew." He kisses my cheek, making Az snarl again but with a little more anger. A loud growl sounds before Rhys is forcefully yanked from me. I see the red-ish demon hoist Rhys onto his hip like a child, but the human just smiles and pets the angry man's chest like one would a disgruntled cat. "Shhh, big guy. You're being too noisy, and I'm trying to talk to my friend." I choke back an incredulous laugh at how much confidence and sass he must have to talk to the giant like that.

"Mine." The demon's voice is crazy low, and his eyes are moving like melted silver. I was able to read Az's books on demon types, so I know this means his sin, one he pointedly calls Wrath, is in control. My heart rate spikes as he glares at me, but when I peek at his soul, I see how connected they are and how gentle he can be. Rhys, oblivious to my momentary panic, just kisses his mate's cheek and addresses us again.

"Yes, I'm his. Aaaand with that understood by all, I would like to introduce you to everyone! This is Wrath. At some point Ari will gain control again and he'll be a little more civil." He pats his mate again and wiggles like he wants down. The demon rolls his eyes

120

and heads inside, only letting him down once he passes through the door. He must say something to Rhys, because the human starts giggling like a schoolboy. I love watching them, as scary as the demon is. Their love gives me hope, and watching their souls interact almost takes my breath away it's so beautiful.

Azvameth nudges me with his elbow, gaining my attention. "Are you okay?" I nod, not quite able to speak yet. Rhys leads us to the open-concept living space and kitchen where I hear more people approaching from the hall and try to brace myself for any reaction. Not all of these encounters will be as nice as Rhys's.

A wisp of a man barrels toward me with a smile on his face. I can see his soul, shredded and sad, so I know the smile is for everyone else's benefit. His body slows when he reaches me, but his soul does not. It seems almost untethered. Unthinkingly, I reach out to touch it, wanting to soothe the ragged edges. I make contact, both of our eyes widening.

"Ivan? What is happening?" Taylor's voice shakes.

"I-I don't know." I ignore being called by the name Constantine gave me and continue to touch his soul, running my hand up and down the side of the shape. Taylor shivers, so I stop immediately.

"Does it hurt?" I ask softly, not wanting to cause him more pain.

"Kind of? Not really a bad hurt, though. Does that make sense?" I shrug. I have no idea. This hasn't happened before.

"What is happening right now? To us it looks like you're petting the air around Tay-Tay. Looks weird as shit." Rhys's comments draw a laugh from everyone and relieves some of the tension I hadn't seen building. I step back, putting my hands in my pockets.

"I would also like to know." Astaroth's voice washes over the room. He seems disgruntled, which is a first from what I've seen.

"I'm not sure. When he ran up to me, I was able to touch his soul. Like physically touch it. I'm truly baffled. I'm sorry, Taylor. I won't do it again." I want to, though. A puzzle I'm dying to get my hands on.

Strong arms wrap around me, and Az's voice relaxes me as he whispers against my ear. "Don't lie, my little scientist. You want answers as much as everyone else does. You'd love to get a chance to study this." He kisses my temple, softening his accusation. He's not wrong, so I shrug, making him chuckle.

"I felt like I *had* to touch it, to help. It seemed to calm his soul even with the little time I had with it. I'd be happy to do it for any of you but won't force anyone, obviously."

"Aaaaanyway. You know Tay-Tay the fae-fae. The two shifters over here trying to become one with the wall

122

are Silas and Beckett. Pip and Selena are in the sunroom, doing witchy things. Dane is around here somewhere, visiting, and Joseph is resting in his room. We had a few others, but they were almost immediately deemed healthy and have since rejoined their families." Rhys switches to me with a sweep of his arm.

"This is Zhenechka. Some of you may know him as Ivan. Anyone uncomfortable may of course retreat to their rooms or the sunroom. We will not be entering there during today's visit." I know the last part was said as a warning to me. Not everyone is comfortable with me being here. A twinge of sorrow moves through me as I nod my acceptance.

I watch as the two men, probably in their twenties, come closer. The timber wolf is taller, with kind brown eyes, dark hair, and tanned skin, while his counterpart is the opposite. Smaller in stature, icy blue eyes, and all hard angles like his artic wolf form. The brunet holds out his hand as if to shake mine. "I'm Beckett. We didn't meet for very long, so don't be embarrassed for not remembering."

"Ah, thank you. I'm glad we didn't meet for long, honestly." I give a sheepish smile. A snort comes from the blond, making shame curl around me. I address Silas. "I know it doesn't make up for it, but I truly am sorry you suffered by my hand."

"Enough of that. No one here blames you. You were compelled, Zhenechka. Let's get to the rest of today.

Franco tells me you were looking for Dane about a renovation project?" Astaroth guides the conversation seamlessly. My shoulders sag in relief as Azvameth takes over explaining what we want to do with the house. I sit back and study Silas and Beckett a bit more, peeking at their souls' state and shivering at what I find. Silas's soul is screaming in pain, trying to separate from his body, thrashing around. I'm horrified at the sight of the thin threads holding him together.

I step forward involuntarily and keep my voice low as to not startle him. My hands itch, and I know I can help if he trusts me just a little. "Silas, I know you don't trust me, but I feel an overwhelming urge to touch you. Not you, you, but your soul. Will you allow me to soothe it like I did for Taylor?"

Panic is evident on his face, but he swallows roughly and looks at Taylor, who gives him an encouraging nod. He looks at me again and steps forward slightly, eyes boring into mine. His soul continues to thrash until I make contact. I keep my movements slow and my touch gentle.

Everything seems to happen at once. A rush of power leaves me, and though I have no idea what's happening, I allow my magic to do what needs to be done. The screaming I alone heard stops, and his soul quivers under the weight of my power. My hand starts to shake and my vision blurs, but I grit my teeth and refuse to let go because his soul has already brightened a few shades, its pain slowly receding. Power continues to pour out of me and into him.

My body trembles with effort, and I register the thudding sound of muffled shouts threatening to break my concentration. I do not have full control, but I know I have to focus on what's happening with Silas so I may be able to understand the motivation of the energy rushing through me. I do know letting go of the soul right now would be catastrophic, so I hold on tighter and continue to let my golden power drain out of me. I know I'll pass out soon, but I'm not worried. I trust Azvameth will catch me.

Chapter Eleven

Azvameth

Zhen doesn't seem to hear us clamoring for him to stop whatever he's doing. Silas is swaying on his feet, and my mate looks close to passing out. Beckett whimpers that Z is hurting Silas, but it doesn't look that way to me. I notice Zhen is frozen in that spot when I try to pull him behind me, so I place myself between my mate and the chaos heading our way. Although I won't hurt any of them intentionally, I will not allow anyone to harm my precious mate. Astaroth hovers in the corner, clearly torn on what to do. A piercing whistle breaks through the shouting, and we all turn toward Rhys.

"He's not hurting him! Look! Look at Silas's face. His coloring is better now than it has been since we found him."

It's true, the man does look healthier than when we arrived, but my mate does not. His pallor is concerning, and tears are streaming down his face, his mouth twisted in pain. Now that the outside threat to my mate has lessened, I start to worry about the danger he's posing to himself. His legs shake, and a gasp leaves the group collectively as his hand finally falls away from where it had been clenching the air around Silas. I catch him before he hits the ground, but his shallow breathing terrifies me.

What the fuck just happened?

"He needs blood, Azvameth. We don't have any here, but I could give him my wrist again."

A low growl leaves me at Astaroth's offer. My mate will only be feeding from me. I slip my wrist against his mouth, but he makes no move to bite me. Fuck. I quickly bite myself, breaking the skin deep enough to allow blood to trickle from the wound at a decent pace before I hover it over his mouth. "C'mon, Z, drink. Please."

His eyes pop open after my blood coats his tongue. He leans forward slightly, suctioning his lips over the bite, dragging large pulls from me. He can take as much as he needs, though getting on an iron supplement might be beneficial in case this happens again. The feeding doesn't incite either pleasure or pain. Maybe it's because he didn't use his fangs to bite me himself. I file that question away for later. Now is definitely not the time to ask about theoretical blood orgasms.

I run my hands over the side of his face and down his neck in a soothing gesture, leaning down and kissing his forehead. The wild look in his eyes lessens, and I see awareness hit him as he takes a final swallow, licking my wound closed almost reverently. "Thank you, *babochka*."

"Anytime, Z." I give him a wink to reinforce that I enjoyed feeding him. I would be happy if he never had to use bagged blood again.

"Not to break up this . . . well, whatever this bite-y thing is, but for the second time today . . . WHAT THE FUCK WAS THAT?!" Rhys's voice ends in a shout, making Zhen flinch, drawing a low growl from my chest. Aridam grumbles back and yanks his mate into his arms with a warning look in my direction.

I steady Zhen as he tries to stand, keeping a hand to his lower back to lend support until he's steady on his feet. His voice is stronger but still exhausted as he tries to explain. He's not sure what happened, but his soul magic did something on its own and fed into Silas.

I'm struck again with how special my mate is. Soul mages used to be incredibly rare, but after hundreds of years we believe that Zhen is the only one remaining. I'm in awe of how much power he must have had as a dual mage to still retain his soul gift even after his transition into a vampire.

"How do you feel, Silas?" Beckett's soft voice cuts through some of the noise, and we all listen intently for his answer.

"Umm, weird? I don't know how to describe it. I feel lighter somehow. Like an angry fog was lifted, if that makes sense." He sounds unsure, but he's not dead so he must be fine. Meh, he'll figure it out. His emotions aren't my problem. I focus my attention again on my little scientist and wait for him to turn and meet my eyes.

"You okay, Z? You had me worried there for a second." I try to keep my tone light to hide my concern, but I apparently fail because he scoffs a little and nods, drawing a wide smile from me.

"I'm just fine, *babochka*. Better than fine, actually. Thank you."

"Holy shit, is Azvameth *smiling*?! Alert someone, alert everyone!" I scowl. Leave it to Rhys to ruin every sweet moment we've had since our arrival.

I toss my best glare his way, but it doesn't seem to affect him by the dopey look he's sporting. I narrow my eyes further at the sight of a phone in his hand. Did he take a picture? I want to smack it out of his hand, but Wrath would pull my entrails out through my nose if I acted on that impulse, so I settle for a good sneer. "Go away." Rhys just cackles in response, and I hear a few phones vibrate around me. No. He didn't. "Did you send that to the team?!" Now I'm alarmed. The others will needle me about this incessantly.

A loud laugh cuts through my growing agitation, and I swing my gaze to meet my mate's. The joy on his face washes away any anxiety about teasing from my team and replaces it with a bolt of arousal. I want to taste that smile. My thoughts must be broadcasting clearly, because Z's breath catches in his throat and his pupils widen. The tip of his tongue darts out of his perfect mouth and wets his lush lower lip.

Without looking away from my mate, I open a portal back to the hotel. I do not stop to say goodbye or give stupid excuses. Let everyone draw their own conclusions. I don't care.

I slam my mouth onto his the second we clear the bedroom, swallowing his gasp and groaning at the heady taste of my own blood mixing with the underlying sweetness of my mate. Goosebumps erupt over my forearms as he slides his hand up the back of my neck, causing me to shiver. A possessive rumble leaves me, and he melts, not even trying to hold

129

himself up. Those needy whimpers escaping him set me on fire, pushing me to lose what control I have.

He's submitting so beautifully, but I don't think he knows what he's asking me for, so I rip my mouth from his, searching his glassy light-green eyes. I refuse to drop my gaze to his swollen mouth, knowing it would wipe every responsible thought from my mind. "What do you need, sweetheart? I'm close to throwing you down, tying you up, and using you within an inch of your life, but I need to know you want this. Say yes and I'll take care of everything—all you need to do is listen to me and feel good. I want to claim you, Zhenechka. I don't want to wait another day to make you mine. Is that what you want too?"

"Yes! *Plez*, yes . . . please!" His begging becomes almost frantic.

Kissing his jaw softly, I let my breath ghost over his ear as I whisper, "Shhh. I'll make this so good for you, sweetheart. Look at you, so needy, so perfect." Leaning back, I grasp the bottom of his shirt and lift it enough to expose his toned torso, groaning at the soft feel of his skin. I continue to gently undress him, taking my time to lavish every newly exposed inch with open-mouthed kisses and slow licks. I need him to understand that this is more than sex. More than getting off. He's everything.

Once my mate is beautifully naked, I lay him on the bed, keeping up the stream of praise he deserves. Pride fills me as I realize he hasn't said anything coherent for quite a while. He obviously enjoys my control. Zhen writhes on the bed, unable to keep still like I want, so I wrap my hands around his wrists and pull them above his head while I wedge myself between his powerful thighs. His legs splay open without any resistance, knees falling to the side. Our groins press tightly together as I rest my full weight on him.

"Keep your hands right here, sweetheart. Don't move them, okay?" He starts nodding before I finish my sentence, and I reward his enthusiasm with a soft kiss. His mouth chases mine for a moment after I pull back. His innocent desperation is doing wicked things to my arousal. I let myself transition to my demon form, watching his eyes widen as my wings spring free. His hands clench and release like he wants to grab me, but he keeps them where they are . . . because he's fucking perfect.

Taking his reaction as encouragement, I allow my tail to trail its feathers up his thigh. His muscles quiver under the sensation, his abdomen clenching in an effort to keep still. As the tail continues its path forward, the feathers catch the tip of his nipple, causing him to gasp. The feathers turn sharp before my tail retraces its journey. I'm rewarded with a low moan and a shiver as the feathers nick his creamy skin above his ribs. The blood rises to the surface of the cuts, but they don't well or drip, closer to papercuts than actual wounds. I know the sting is just this side of painful, and my mate is reveling in it. His love of a little pain with his pleasure fills me with a desperation I've never felt before. I watch as the feathers catch on his nipple, causing him to cry out in surprise and arch his back.

My control slips, and I attack his mouth with my own, sucking, biting, and licking every inch I can access. I swallow his moans as I use my free hand to open his cheeks, rubbing his hole with my thumb. Fumbling to get the lube without breaking contact with his mouth is frustrating as fuck and takes me longer than if I had just pulled away to grab it, but I won't give him a single breath to reconsider his plea. I cover my fingers as quickly as possible while distracting him with my tail. His ass is hot and tight, gripping me hard enough it might actually hurt my dick when I enter him. The knowledge that I'm his first turns me into a caveman, but I cannot help but revel in it.

"Whose ass is this, sweetheart?" Up to two fingers now, I still my arm so he can collect himself enough to respond.

"You-yours! *Babochka,* please!"

"Do you want another finger, or do you want to hurt more for me?" I didn't know I wanted that until it came from my mouth unbidden, but now that I've said it, I find it's true. His pain is so sweet when it's just for me, and he clearly loves the idea—the spasming around my fingers tells me so.

"No more waiting. Get in me! I need you—fuck!" I notch the head of my cock into his opening, torn between watching his body accept mine and watching his face as I enter him. My choice is made for me when he closes his eyes. I need to watch those green eyes as I fuck my mate for the first time.

"Open! I need to see those beautiful eyes, sweetheart. Lemme see." His eyes sluggishly open, taking no small amount of effort. "There you go. Good boy." He whimpers at the praise.

I push my hips forward, letting the tightening around his eyes guide me. I want it to burn but not actually hurt him. Cupping his face, I use my thumb to drop his jaw, leaving his lips parted. I bend to swipe my tongue over his open mouth before setting a punishing pace with my hips. I want to hear every sound he makes, so I keep my thumb on his chin. I want to simply rut into him and bite, but I need to watch at least one orgasm overtake him before I allow myself to claim him. His eyes lose focus, and I feel the start of his orgasm in the fluttering of his ass, so I lean back to take his angry red cock in hand, squeezing a little too hard before stroking him even harder, my thrusts never letting up their punishing pace.

"Give it to me, sweetheart. Come for me, mate." As if on cue, he explodes. The grip he has on my cock almost makes my vision white out, but I hold on. Tears escape his glassy eyes, and he sobs his way through his orgasm. After I'm sure his orgasm has been milked for as long as possible, I use his languid body like a sleeve to chase my own release. A tingle forms in the base of my spine, giving me a few seconds' warning before it crashes through me. No slow buildup, just overwhelming pleasure. I use the hand still on his jaw to turn his head to the side before striking. His high-pitched moan accompanies another orgasm for both of us. I take a swallow of my mate's blood and pull back, licking the wound.

Our bond settles over me gently but firmly, almost like a weighted blanket. Security and love flow through me as our eyes meet, and I know he's feeling the same way. He smiles softly before tipping his face up, silently asking for a kiss. I give in, plundering lazily with no intent to arouse, only looking to bask in the intimacy of the moment. His mouth slackens slightly and his neck muscles relax, confusing me for a moment before I realize my mate fell asleep. I laugh lightly before pulling the blankets that had fallen off the bed during our mating over us, tucking him in. I allow my human form to come forward so I can rest my head on his chest comfortably, lulled to sleep by his even breaths.

Chapter Twelve

Zhen

The weight on my chest is foreign as I wake, but the feeling is comforting. I breathe in Azvameth's scent, loving the peace it gives me paired with the feeling of the new bond in my chest. A twinge from my ass reminds me that I'm no longer a virgin, and though I love the soreness from our coupling, I'm not a fan of the feeling of dried ejaculate on my skin. Very odd.

Trying not to wake my mate, I slip from under him and bolt to the bathroom to wash off. I can't help but replay last night in my mind while the water warms. My sloth demon was attentive and domineering in the best way. It's always enlightening to learn new things about oneself, so I don't shy away from the knowledge that I seemed to crave the pain Az gave me. My body responded without my say so last night. Normally that would send me into a tizzy—I hate not being in control of my faculties—but apparently in the bedroom I am quite content to let go. Fascinating. I wonder what else I will enjoy.

I read in one of Az's books that sloth demons like extreme sex. My mate told me it wasn't the same with me, and while I enjoy being special to him, maybe I want to see what my own limits are.

I continue to let my mind wander as I wash up, making sure to get everything as clean as possible in case Az wakes up hungry for more than breakfast. I can feel him stirring through the bond, and I'm feeling a bit peckish myself, so I dry off as quickly as possible before walking back to the bedroom with the towel around my waist.

"What a lovely view to wake up to, my mate. Though there does seem to be something in the way of my favorite bits." Az's teasing tone makes me smile.

"Ah, so you wish for me to be naked? Always or just right now? I can't imagine you want your team to see me nake—umph!" My own teasing is cut off as Az yanks me onto the bed, pressing his lips to mine to silence me before pulling back.

"You can walk around as you wish. Be naked all the time if that's what you want. I'll simply kill anyone who looks at you." He sounds serious, but he is also smiling, so I'm confused. I try gauging it from the bond, but his feelings are also harder to decipher than I thought they'd be. Best to assume he's serious.

"What?! You can't just kill someone for seeing me naked!"

"Why not?" He seems genuinely confused.

"You shouldn't just go around killing people. What if it's an accident or something?"

"Then I will just pluck out their eyes instead of killing them. Is that better?"

"No. Not better, Azvameth. No plucking, no maiming, no killing . . . unless it's necessary or in self-defense or something."

"So picky. Fine. I guess you'll just have to be clothed outside of our room, then. To preserve the lives you claim are so sacred." He smirks at me, and I realize I've been played.
I smack his shoulder. "Very funny."

"Do not be mistaken, little scientist; I would absolutely carry out my threat. You're just so sexy when you're feeling scandalized." I scowl at his humor, and it just makes him chuckle. Impossible man.

"Have you checked your phone this morning? We did leave yesterday rather abruptly." Good change of topic. Now he just has to take the bait.

"No, why would I? I'm not going to apologize for carting you off like a caveman. I will be doing so often, so they can get used to it. I do not like sharing your time with others, little scientist. Your work is one thing, but other beings grate on my skin. Why do you need to spend time with things that breathe? It's so annoying."

He's whining. A sloth demon is whining about sharing. I'm now convinced my mate is just a murderous puppy. I shouldn't find him adorable, but I do. I also have to nip this isolation idea in the bud now before he runs with it.

"Well, after so long without real contact, I would like to make a few friends. I don't think I'll have too many because of my past, but maybe Rhys if his mate doesn't squish me? Lily is an odd duck, but I quite like her. Would she be a good choice of friend?"

His eyes soften at my questions, and he leans in for a gentle kiss. "Anyone would be lucky to be your friend, sweetheart. I'll . . . *try* not to be so selfish with you, but no promises. I require a lot of kisses from my mate if he's insistent on having *friends*." He deliberately makes it sound like having friends is absolutely disgusting, but his eyes twinkle.

"Why thank you, *babochka*. I'll make sure to ply you with plenty of kisses whenever we have to interact with people." I kiss his chin and hop off the bed quickly before he can pull me back and distract me from my original question. "Now, you need to check your phone and get ready. I want to pop back to the safe house to see if Dane is there, and we need to talk to Astaroth to see what the plan is with the souls and how I tie into it all."

He grumbles from his spot on the bed, jerking the covers away before climbing off the bed and stomping to find his phone. I myself find that I have missed a few calls from Astaroth and a couple from unknown numbers. No voicemails, so I check my texts and find one from Rhys.

Rhys: *Hey! It's Rhys! I have a million and ten questions to ask you later. Not right now obviously . . . I will behave and wait until you talk to Astaroth before hunting you down and making you my other bestie. Ari says that I have to give you a few days to figure shit out. I'm not happy about waiting, but I depend on the man for most of my orgasms so I'll be good and listen.*

I laugh out loud at the inappropriate ramblings and read on to the next text that came in only a minute later.

Rhys: *I was told that my last text was TMI. I think they're wrong, because Ari is being stuffy and a little stingy with sexy time gossip, to be honest. Any guy who has tail skills like that should be suggesting I brag about our sex life, not hide it. What do you think?*

I tap out a reply conveying my confusion.

Me: *What do I think of the TMI in the first message or about bragging about tail things and sex lives?*

Rhys: *Yes.*

See? This is the kind of thing I need clarified. It sounds like a trap to me, so I'll go with a vague answer.

Me: *I think both parties should agree on what is TMI and how open you would like to be as a couple about sexual activities when talking to others. Maybe?"*

Rhys: *Hmmm. You're right. Consent is sexy. Hold, please, while I ask him.*

What? Okay, I really don't need an update, but I guess I'll be getting one anyway.

Strong arms wrap around my midsection as Az reads over my shoulder. He huffs when he sees the text thread. "Just so you know, you can brag about me and my tail whenever you want, sweetheart." I feel myself flush. It *was* a good tail. He continues, saving me from having to formulate a response. "I won't tell anyone anything specific if you don't want me to, but my scent will probably say a whole lot, and I'm not sorry about it." He runs his nose from my mating mark to under my ear, causing me to shiver.

My phone sounds in my hand. Instead of Rhys's follow-up text, I'm getting a call from Astaroth. I hurry to answer, putting him on speaker so I don't have to lean away from Az's attention on my neck. He must have seen who was calling, but he doesn't stop his light torture on my senses.

"Zhen? Are you there?" Concern flows through the line.

"Ahem, yup. Yep. Here. I mean . . . yes. I'm here." I'm a bumbling idiot, that's what I am. A little nibble on my jaw and I go from scientist to sex fiend.

"Azvameth, let the poor man concentrate. I assume you're the reason this normally brilliant and put-together professional just said 'yup'?"

I groan in embarrassment because I know my mate has no shame. I cut in before Az has a chance to respond with something highly inappropriate. "What can I do for you, sir?"

"I would like to see you at the safe house in an hour. Beckett has agreed to be the next guinea pig in our attempt to figure out what happens when you make contact with their souls. I can't say I understand it, but we need to focus some of our efforts on this instead of just hunting the other big players in Constantine's plan.

"I have the beta teams ready to take over recognizance for those we know the names of, and we have Orobas's trial next week for his involvement. I understand Belial and Kieran have taken that part over, so there's no need for us to come up with a way for you to be present, Zhenechka. You cannot enter Hell, and quite frankly I cannot allow Orobas out of it. He will die after the trial, so I'm only concerned for the next week that he will be able to send someone after you. Keep on your toes, Azvameth.

"Anyway, back on track. I believe it would be in everyone's best interest if you focus on your soul power and how it can help those souls we've rescued. Start with the ones at the house, and then we can travel to those who have already returned home. Does this sound good to the both of you?"

I hesitate. "Do you want me to also set aside my research for the time being?" I would hate that, but this does seem more important.

"Oh no, dear boy. Your research is fundamental to supe development, and I won't have you stop when it means so much to you. You may need to pull back how many hours you spend per week on it to balance with the soul work, but you should continue as much as you feel comfortable," Astaroth reassures me.

"Then I'm good."

"Azvameth? Are you comfortable handing off your leads and information to the beta teams? They are just compiling information and tracking the names your mate gave so we know if they will make a move. I will get together with Aridam when we get closer to putting a plan in place for a takedown."

"That's fine. I would be more comfortable going with my mate and protecting him while he works. The bond really doesn't like the idea of leaving him when there could be a real threat to his life." He kisses my temple almost in apology before talking directly to me instead of the duke. "I believe you can defend yourself, Z. I just don't think I can leave you right now."

I smile at him. "That's okay, *babochka*. I completely understand."

A clap sounds over the speaker. "Perfect. See you two in a little less than an hour." Astaroth hangs up quickly after that, no doubt busy getting the pieces in place now that we have a rough plan.

Azvameth

"You're looking better today, Silas. How do you feel?" Z's tone is soothing, but the little blond is frosty as always. That little shit. I can't help but glare. If he so much as hurts my gentle mate's feelings, I will have no choice but to maim him. I thought he'd be smarter, but the little wolf is *such* an asshole. Honestly I would normally find his frigid non-responses funny if it involved anyone else, but directed at Z it just pisses me off.

I keep part of my attention on my mate as I watch my team gather outside the safe house through the bay window. The excited looks on Belial's and Kieran's faces worry me a bit. They look way too happy to be here. Then I spot Rhys behind them, *skipping* toward the house. Suspicious as fuck. He reaches the front door first, pulling it open with drama.

"Oh, honeykins! I have people here who are just dying to meet you!" His manic smile is pointed at Z, making me pull him closer. My mate just chuckles at our antics, but his eyes warily scan the rest of the team.

"Hello, Zhenechka. I'm Belial and this is Kieran. We're so excited to meet you formally. I've heard a lot about you." The envy demon's voice is a little nervous, no doubt concerned about his effect on people. My mate's smile widens to fill his face, and his eyes turn glassy.

"Z?" Did something happen and I just didn't see it? "He's so beautiful, *babochka*."

The fuck?

"Excuse me?!" I sound as affronted as I am.

"His soul is so beautiful; I wish you could see what I see." He hasn't taken his eyes off Bel, a single tear escaping when he blinks. Belial blushes, but his small smile makes my heart squeeze. Bel needs more friends, and I think my mate just decided to adopt him.

Kieran pushes Belial and Rhys aside to greet Zhen. "Oh my gosh, hi. I wanted to meet you when I brought Lily to your place, but your mate was being a dick and said you needed more time. I mean, if you did, then fine, but I think he just wanted to keep you to himself a bit longer. You're adorable. And I know I won't affect you as much as I will a human, so I'm excited I don't have to stay away from you like I have to with Rhys now. I want to hug you. Can I hug you?!" Kieran bounces from foot to foot like he has to pee.

They said Kieran makes Rhys weird now, so I had wondered how they were handling that. I wasn't worried about his effect on my little scientist since he's a supernatural, but I catch Rhys wiggling next to Belial and looking around for someone. I assume he's looking for Aridam. I can't help but chuckle at his obvious discomfort with being aroused around everyone.

"Yes, hug the vampire, Kieran. See how that works out for you." Kek's judgy voice comes from the doorway. Zhen flinches, and pain flares in my chest from the bond at the implied insult. I'll kill him. I make it two steps closer, but before I can slit his throat for hurting my mate, Ari smacks the back of his head hard enough to give Kek whiplash.

"Shut up, Kek. We've discussed this. Get over it or leave. Better yet, I'll let my kitten have a go at you." We swing our gazes to Rhys, and Kek shrinks back forcefully. Rhys's face is red with rage. Kieran's hand covers his mouth, but we can tell his muffled shouts are actually threats. Based on his hand motions, I'm assuming he's threatening to shove unpleasant things up Kek's ass. What's funny is Kek could snap Rhys in half without a thought, but he's terrified of the little Null—we all are. Wrath would find immense joy in holding any of us down for actual torture just to please Rhys, so we tend to cater to the sassy thing he calls a mate.

"It's okay. I understand where he's coming from. I don't expect everyone to forget. I have agreed to stop apologizing for it, though, so I will not be doing that. Feel how you feel, pride demon. It won't affect my life much, but the bitterness may affect yours. Now if you will excuse me, I want to work with Beckett and Silas today. I'm assuming the white demon behind Kek is Devland. To get a better picture, I would like very much to get your take on what happened right after the souls came with you. Is that acceptable to you?" Devland just smiles at Zhen and nods, following him when Z turns and leaves with the two broken wolves.

I walk to follow them, removing my blade as I go. Reaching the doorway, I turn and throw the knife at Kek. It sinks into his shoulder with a thud, and I smile in satisfaction. Warning issued, I continue my walk to my mate, only just catching Kieran's words before I'm out of hearing range. "You deserved that, Kek. You're lucky it was just a regular blade and not obsidian."

Entering the backyard after the group, I find them setting up yoga mats. Excitement runs through me. Neither I nor my dick will complain if I get to see my bulky mate be all bendy. Instead, everyone sits and they start *meditating*. I'm sure it's super helpful, but meditating is a long four-letter word. Why would you want to just *sit and think*? Gross. I try to listen to Z's soothing voice, but the only thing that happens is an inappropriate tenting in my pants and a laser focus on my mate's mouth. It's just so pretty.

"Az, do you want to do a perimeter check?" I hear the poorly disguised laughter in Aridam's voice, but I can't blame him. I didn't hear him come out because I was too busy obsessing over Zhen. I wince, knowing the main reason I'm here is for Z's protection. Good thing Ari isn't a bad guy. Oops. I just give him a quick nod and run away before Zhen's sexiness draws me back into a trance.

Chapter Thirteen

Zhen

I open my eyes, feeling more centered, and glance to where Az was standing before we started. Where did he go? Surveying the area, I come up empty. I look to Devland and furrow my eyebrows with the unspoken question.

"He's checking out the area. He'll be back soon. Do you need me to grab him?"

Of course he didn't just leave. Get ahold of yourself. I shake my head, both at myself and to answer the greed demon. "No, I don't blame him for his need to move around. He doesn't need to watch me sit here, let alone participate. I doubt he could be still long enough without distracting everyone else anyway."

My assessment makes him chuckle. "Well, if you need anything, just let me know . . . or shout. Aridam is distracting his mate inside, but he'll come out if you yell. Actually Rhys is chomping at the bit to get out here, but I think he would be more of a distraction for you guys than help."

I almost laugh, but I'm not quite confident enough to do so where Aridam might hear. I like my insides right where they are. I turn my attention to the pair of wolves in front of me, trying to get back on track.

"How did that feel for you guys?" I make sure to look at their souls as they answer, wanting to see any differences in their movements. Silas's moves less violently but isn't anywhere near healthy. Beck's soul has also been mauled, but it seems almost subdued and sad. How interesting.

"I didn't really feel anything. It was boring, but I tried my best." Beck's soft voice draws gentle smiles from everyone in the group, Devland included. I rush to reassure him.

"It's like that at first. It's a pain, but doing it every day will put you more in tune with your body and your wolf. I admit I'm not well versed in the relationship between shifters and their animals, only the science of it."

"Oh! It's actually just me. Like there is me as a wolf and me as more human. When I'm a wolf, the small human worries kind of melt away and I'm driven more by instinct, but it's not like there's another person inside of me."

"That explains why I only see one consciousness in your soul. Good. I was worried your wolf had been separated from you somehow. Good to know. Silas? How about you? How are you feeling?" He just grunts in response. I wait patiently to see if he'll add something more eventually.

"Fine. No better or worse." An elbow from Beck has him adding a quick and almost sincere-sounding thanks. I accept the prickly response, knowing that's just how the man is.

"I'm going to be honest. I still don't know what I'm doing, but if you'd like to help me figure it out?" I kind of trail off. "I just want to help."

A shirtless Azvameth interrupts my guilt spiral by sliding in next to me like he's stealing home plate. The amount of energy he has when he's excited is crazy.

"Have a good time, *babochka*?"

"Yes! Do you know how long a wolf can run at top speed? So cool. I've never raced a wolf before, and now I want to race all of them. I'm pretty sure Dane thought I would be easy to beat, but even he was panting hard by the end." His eyes hold a maniacal gleam, and a fine sheen of sweat covers his skin.

"How come you get to walk around shirtless but I don't?" It doesn't seem fair. I do enjoy the view, but maybe I want to be the only one enjoying it.

"You can go shirtless whenever you want, my little scientist. We already had this conversation, remember?" My eyes widen as I remember his threat. While seeing him spar would make me rock hard in seconds, I shouldn't let him know how much the idea turns me on.

"Did you guys want us to leave? I'm getting all hot and bothered over here." Devland's comment pulls a giggle from Beck and a disgusted scoff from Silas. I completely forgot they were there.

I see Az snap his teeth at our audience, Silas in particular, and I know he's only half joking, so I rush to get our conversation back to safer ground. "All right. Now, Beck, I was thinking it would be best to just observe your soul for a while and save the touching for when my magic pushes me to." Oh! That gives me an idea. "Az! Did you happen to bring my recorder?"

"Umm . . . no? I can quickly grab it from the house if you need it." He readies his body, but Devland interrupts.
"You know you can use the voice recording app on your phone, though, right?" His voice is laced with humor.

I flush, embarrassed for not thinking about it. I'm trying to get better at technology and the cool things my phone can do, but obviously there are some things I miss . . . regularly. I clear my throat and pull my phone out of my pocket. I forget it's there ninety percent of the time, only looking at it when it makes a noise and Az isn't next to me. My mate snakes his hand behind me to smack the back of Devland's head hard enough his teeth clack together. He glares at Az with a promise of retribution.

"Thank you. I, ahem, didn't think about that. Sorry." Both wolves snicker, though I don't think they're making fun of me. I press on, knowing if Az sees me

151

upset any longer it will just start an actual fight. "I want to record what I'm seeing in real time so I can revisit it. It would be helpful to hear my thoughts as they come instead of trying to remember every detail later. Are you okay with that, Beck?"

"For sure! Doesn't matter to me."

Perfect. I make sure it's all set up so I can just focus on the wolf in front of me. Silas and Devland scoot back to give us some space, watching us intently. Azvameth settles behind me, letting me lean against him slightly in a show of support. Though he pulls his phone out and plays on it, I know he's paying very close attention. Both Beck and Silas sag in relief, so I'm glad he knows he makes the wolves a little tense every time he looks at them too long. I'll have to talk to him about threatening people less and how he could make more friends by smiling at more than just me. Baby steps.

I adjust my eyes and take in Beck's soul. I make sure to keep up a running monologue of every thought and detail I come across, not worrying about rambling or whether something is important or not. I tune my own voice out and focus solely on the damaged soul itself. Listless, it just sways around Beckett. I continue staring, waiting for any indication that I should touch it. I don't feel the same overwhelming urge like I did with Taylor and Silas. Should I touch it anyway? I don't feel like I shouldn't, so I carefully lift my right hand to hover close to the soul. There's no pull or push of my power, so I get closer, touching it. Cool and calm, the soul pushes into my hand like a cat demanding pets. I oblige, petting firmly but not hard. I hear a choked laugh, probably from calling a wolf a cat, but I ignore it.

The soul soaks up the attention, but there's no draw on my power. Perhaps I need to use some intention? I focus on how I might be able to help him. He's such a sweet man; I wish I could heal him even a little. I know it has to be painful, not being whole. A soft glow collects around my hand, and I gasp as it connects gently to the soul, touching the places it's torn. I watch, mystified, as it starts to knit together. Why is this so much different from the other times? I don't feel drained, but I can see some of my power trickling into the soul.

I don't want to push too hard. Knowing that healing too fast can cause more harm than good, I slowly retract my hand, pulling away the golden light. Adjusting my vision again to Beck's face, I catch a serene smile and a tear falling before I'm pulled into Azvameth's lap. I wait until Beck opens his watery brown eyes before I speak, wanting to give him time to come back to reality.

"How are you feeling?" I ask softly.

His smile stretches, and he blinks more tears away. "Thank you. I feel better, more settled. I don't feel whole, but like a missing part of me was given back. Thank you, Zhen." He sobs and turns into Silas's arms, hugging him tightly. The little blond isn't glaring at me, so he must be happy for his friend.

"Are you saying you're actually healing their souls? This is huge, my little scientist. They'll be whole again?"

"I don't know how long it will take, but yes, I believe I can. There will be a huge difference on how much power it takes if the soul was shredded and they're still alive versus if they've already died." Everyone freezes and looks at me. I stop recording.

"Wait. You think you can heal the souls stuck at Reception?! Truly?" I nod. "Shit, I need to call Astaroth . . . and Ari . . . shit, and the angels!" Devland recovers from his shock and jumps up, sprinting to the house.

The remaining members of our group continue to stare at me with varying degrees of awe. I start to squirm under their collective gaze, my discomfort growing. Azvameth snaps out of it and pulls me into his lap, kissing behind my ear and whispering reassuring nonsense.

The grumpy scowl that overtakes Silas's face as he watches us is so fierce it breaks the tension. Beck laughs. "Let's give them some privacy before the demon takes offense to your face." They gather themselves and walk away, still bickering.

I focus back on my mate, slightly nervous. It would help if I could feel more things through the bond. I can tell he's not upset, but I can't narrow it down more than that. I read about the shallow feelings sloth demons have been known to have, but Az told me he has been feeling more since meeting me. I want to ask him questions, but I don't know if they'll be well received. He must feel my curiosity, which is so incredibly unfair. He just waits with his best questioning face. I sigh and explain what I have been thinking.

"Well, I feel deeper than I had before, and they're more complex. It's confusing more than anything, but actually feeling what you do through the bond helps. I didn't know what I was feeling before, so feeling anything at all used to make me . . . agitated. I don't know if that's the right word. Annoyed? Bored? Frustrated? It's easier for me to identify the small things because I can use our bond as a reference and you can explain it if I don't understand. It doesn't help me cope with actually feeling them, but being able to feel you in here"—he pats his chest—"makes it worth it."

Der'mo, why is he so sweet? "I didn't know that. You know you can always ask me how I'm feeling or what is making me feel a certain way. I'll always be honest with you, even if it's hard to explain. Would it help for me to say out loud what I'm feeling so you can match it to what you feel through the bond?"

"Hmmm . . . I don't know. I kind of like having to figure it out, but I don't want to guess something wrong and have it hurt or upset you." His brow crinkles in worry.

I try to push affection through our bond, and his face lights up, blue eyes twinkling. He kisses my forehead, cuddling my too-large-for-this frame.

"We'll figure it out, *babochka*." I let him have his cuddle time, not knowing what we should be doing next. I wiggle, feeling him harden beneath me. Sitting on his lap should feel weird with us being the same size, but it just feels right.

"If you don't want me to strip you right here, little scientist, you have to stop moving around." His grumble makes me huff in amusement. I know he's not kidding, but I also know we won't be uninterrupted for long, so I make no move to stop.

Like I predicted, I am only able to rile up my mate for another minute before Devland runs back toward us holding a phone while the other demons I met this morning follow at a more sedate pace.

"Hey, Z! Astaroth has questions!" He thrusts the phone at me as he reaches us. "It's on speaker."

"Good afternoon, Zhenechka. I apologize for interrupting you on your second day, but needs must. Devland told me what you said earlier. I would like to test your theory sooner rather than later. I understand adding another thing to your plate will push your research further behind. I hope that is acceptable?" His tone doesn't convey a threat or pressure, so I assume he is genuinely asking if I can set aside my research for now and would try to make it work if I refused.

I don't like it, but this is more important only because it's time sensitive. Bloodlust won't go anywhere if I wait. "Of course. What do you need me to do?"

"Sit tight for now. Keep working with the souls at the safe house. I have to coordinate with Gabriel to see if we can get you a pass to go to Reception. I wanted to check to see if you were willing before I called that insufferable angel." A few chuckles escape the team. I assume the duke's distaste for Gabriel is well known amongst them. Makes sense that the leaders of the afterlife wouldn't get along. Wait. Who runs Neutral, then? I make a note to ask Az later.

"Got it, sir. Should I wait to interact with those here at the safe house until after we get permission, or can I still help people in the meantime?" I'm worried he'll ask me to wait to shore up my power reserves. I don't want Beck, Silas, or the others to suffer more because of me.

"No, no. This may take a few days to set up. There's always all of this red tape before anything of importance can actually be done when it involves multiple realms," Astaroth reassures me.

"That's good. Let me know if you need anything else from me in the interim." Azvameth makes his own goodbyes before hanging up.

"Well, shit, you're just full of fun surprises, aren't you?!" Rhys asks, looking excited. "Do you have enough energy to work with more people, or do you want to stick with Beck and Silas for now?"

I consider the pros and cons. "I don't want to make that decision until I get a good look at their souls. It might be slower going for some more than others, but I'm leaning toward doing sessions on rotation until they're all healed. That way everyone gets a little better each week. Is that a good idea or will it start trouble? I'm assuming it won't take as long to heal Beck as it will Silas, but once Beck is done, maybe I could double up on someone else? Should I have a schedule?" Az makes a noise at my question. I turn to watch his face and am surprised to see annoyance. Usually that's not directed at me.

"How will we know what you can handle until you've met everyone? I won't have you hurting yourself trying to heal everyone, little scientist. Your well-being is the priority here." He kisses my nose to gentle the rebuke. I understand his point, but I don't have to like it.

"Well, today I'm feeling up for another session, if that's okay with everyone? Should I go find Silas or do we start with someone new?" I ask Rhys. He seems to be in charge here at the house.

"Let's ask Joseph. He's a cranky old Scottish bastard, but he wasn't held for long. I can put out feelers to the rest here and see if they're willing to meet you yet. Some aren't ready and that's okay. You'll help those willing to accept it."

An air of mystery surrounds his last statement. I must not be the only one confused, because Kieran chimes in. "Why wouldn't someone want help? They've heard of what Zhenechka can do to help them, so why would someone volunteer to still be in pain?"

Rhys shakes his head. "They aren't my reasons to share. Let's just say not everyone was taken from a happy place. They have nowhere to go back to that isn't just as bad as where they were rescued from."

I wonder who he's talking about, but it's none of my business. I stand, offering my hand to Azvameth. "Let's go meet this Joseph."

Chapter Fourteen

Azvameth

We wait for Rhys to bring Joseph to the dining room, once again steering clear of the sunroom to keep it a safe space. I'm curious to see who here at the safe house has had personal contact with Zhen. It didn't sound like Z had met Joseph before, but he may just be trying to protect him. I try to think back on his recordings, but I don't remember a Joseph being one of the names he gave.

A whoosh of air leaves Zhen's lungs like he's been sucker punched, followed by a pained groan. I look around wildly to find the threat, only to see a middle-aged man hobbling into the room behind Rhys. His gait doesn't tell me exactly what's wrong with him, but I gather the damage was done by my mate while under compulsion. Scars cover the right side of his face and neck, continuing under his shirt. His hand on the same side looks mangled. Seeing the damage, I can recall one of the victims Zhen talked about in the recording; he just never knew his name.

"Ach, lad, none of that now. 'M fine. Rhys said you think you can work some magic on my soul?"

"Joseph, I'm so—"

"I won't be hearing no apologies from you, lad. You've done nothing that hadn't already been done before, and you certainly didn't do it cause ye wanted to."

Z takes a second to gather himself, and I see a flash of pride on the man's face when my mate continues like the professional he is. "Yes. To answer your question, I can help heal your soul. The damage is there, but your soul is strong and not in immediate distress. I can explain the process as much as I can before we start, and you can ask questions at any time."

"Nah, I trust ye. I don't want to listen to yer droning on again. I actually got to rest here, ye ken."

Zhen huffs and nods. "You gave quite the performance, then. You let me believe you thought my research was fascinating. You have no idea how much I appreciated it."

"Wait, so you know each other? That's crazy!" Rhys voices my own confusion.

"Ach, yes. The lad here was researching, and I was the unwilling bodyguard while he did so. I was able to break out of the coven with the lad's help but got my arse caught before I could get away myself. Never told him my name because I knew Ivan wasn't his and wanted us on even ground. Then after I was caught, I kept it to myself. There's a big difference between knowing the name of the wolf yer forced to torture and not. Thought I was doing the lad a favor." He gives a self-depreciating smile. "Now I know yours, lad. Zhenechka suits you."

"Thank you, Joseph." There's an awkward pause.

My skin starts to itch. "I'm Azvameth, Zhen's mate. Nice to meet you." I push my hand out to shake his until I realize he may not be able to shake my hand with that amount of scar tissue. Fuck. I just stand there like an idiot, skin itchy and uncomfortable with everyone staring like I've grown a second head. Only Z is trying not to laugh. He pats the hand still suspended in midair and gives me an out.

"Perimeter check time, *babochka*?" His tone is light and teasing, affection flowing through the bond.

"Yes! That. I'll go . . ." I don't bother finishing my sentence, which I spoke at a crazy loud volume for no reason, before scampering away. How embarrassing.

I just make it outside the safe house before Belial appears in front of me, looking excited. "Az! We have a lead on Alpha Gregory. Aaaaaand a date has been set for Orobas's trial."

"Yes! We really needed that lead; Aridam told me how frustrated the beta team is getting. When is the trial?" I hope I can help tackle both, but the trial may take precedence with my mate's testimony being involved. I know Astaroth wanted to keep Z as far away from the traitorous greed demon as possible, but since this affects more than just demons, he may not have the final say.

Why do they get to decide? I'm his mate; I should be in charge of—

"Shit, Belial, I'm sorry. I'm hitting my limit. Do you need me to grab Rhys, or are we good for now?" Envy whips through me more readily than it has before. Maybe because it has to do with my mate? I already don't like someone being able to make decisions about my little scientist, but normally the only place I want to control Z is in the bedroom.

The crestfallen look Bel gives breaks my heart. It used to be that he affected me less than some others because I didn't care about much so there wasn't much envy to push. Having a mate and experiencing *feelings* have changed that. And because of the feelings, I *care* that I hurt his. Dumb. Absolutely ridiculous.

"It's okay, Az. We, uh, I can send you a text with the info. I'm going to head back to the team house . . . Could you tell Rhys?" I don't get a chance to respond as he simply turns and portals away.

Feeling like an asshole, I head out to actually do that perimeter check. I do so on autopilot, looking but not really seeing as I obsess over this feeling. Guilt? Could I have handled that better? I should ask Z when he's done with Joseph. A chime from my phone pulls my attention.

Bel: Orobas's trial is at 9:00 a.m. tomorrow. Astaroth will use Zhenechka's recording in lieu of a live testimony. It will take place in the old HQ building. Are you planning on attending the trial or staying with Zhenechka?

Me: I'll have to talk to him about it. If we decide I should go in person, will you and Rhys stay with him? He's really fond of you both, and I don't want him to be alone.

The three dots that indicate he's typing sit there for quite a while, so I send a follow-up.

Me: Please? I don't think I could leave him otherwise.

Bel: Of course. I'm doing it for him, though, not you.

Me: Understood.

Leaving Zhen is harder than I anticipated. I knew I would struggle, but the pull from my chest is making me feel panicked. It's quite annoying. I know he's fine, but tell that to our bond. It's solid, but our rocky beginning makes it hard to be separated for any length of time. It wants extra reassurance that we aren't fighting, or that's what Astaroth told me earlier. I've talked to more people today than I have in weeks.

I make my way into the makeshift courtroom, staying closer to the back. I let off a trickle of power, wanting to be overlooked just in case there are chatty bad guys also watching from the crowd. The sheer number of people in attendance makes it hard to pick out more than just snippets of conversations. I keep my eyes and ears peeled on the off chance I catch something.

The giant warehouse doors crash open, signaling the arrival of both Orobas and our dear duke. Orobas looks terrible, with dried blood on his face and neck, the injuries caused by obsidian by the looks of them. Obsidian knuckles, probably. They give a lovely bruising pattern with small nicks to slow healing if used at the right angle.

The crowd quiets as Astaroth raises his hands for silence. "Today we are here to bear witness to the trial and sentencing of the high-level greed demon known as Orobas. He has been accused of treason, disregarding direct orders from a duke, breaking his oath as a demon in my ranks, and subterfuge past what is allowed as a demon."

He turns to address the demon directly. "I'm more than ready to hear what you have to say for yourself, Orobas."

I pay attention to the crowd instead of the trial, knowing I'll be caught up later, and unless my mate's name is uttered, I don't really care. Nothing jumps out at me, just random exclamations and murmurs of disbelief. It's not until I hear someone mention Felicity that I home in on the two greed demons a few yards away from me. Only our team, Astaroth, and Zhen know about Felicity's involvement. These demons are low level, making me think they got pulled in under Orobas to do some of his dirty work. I make sure my power is leaking at the perfect level for me to slip over behind them unseen, opening a portal behind me. I wait until the crowd gets loud again to cover any noise they might make and grab them, throwing us all through the portal.

The Colorado coven house has become my interrogation space for this assignment, so I instinctively brought them here. I'm able to throw them into the nullifying cell before they wiggle away. I pull out my phone to text the beta team I'm working closest with that they have some company here.

I hear their arrival moments later. "Hey, Azvameth! Got one?"

"Two, actually. You got them? I'd like to head back and collect more if needed."

The pride demon's eyebrows rise in offense, and he looks to his envy demon partner in disbelief. Envy just rolls his eyes before taking over and answering my question. "Yeah, man. We got this. You do you."

I can't remember what his name is . . . something short. Shack? That's wrong, but I never cared enough to learn the envy demon's name before.

"Thanks . . .?" Thankfully he catches on with a grin.

"No worries, man. I'm Shax and this is Helel." Helel seems even more affronted that I didn't remember his name but wisely chooses to say nothing. Pride is tricky like that.

I just nod and portal back, releasing my power back to a trickle to avoid notice. Unfortunately I've missed a large portion of the trial just by talking with the beta team members. It looks like it's at its end, just waiting

166

for the punishment and verdict from our duke. I spy Allocer and know he's going to be the one carrying out the sentence.

"As a shadowling, you can at least do something useful and help power Hell. I hand you off to Allocer, who I know will take the very best care of you." Astaroth's sugary sarcasm is sharp and venomous.

The duke in charge of the shadowlings and truly depraved souls . . . smiles? It's more of a grimace but whatever floats the deranged fucker's boat. I doubt he has too many reasons to smile in a non-creepy-as-fuck way, so I try to ignore how he always makes my skin crawl.

I stay behind to listen for more chatter but come up with nothing. Maybe Orobas's operation was small on this side. It doesn't seem like his part was all that big in the grand scheme. Smart because one should never trust a demon unless they give their word. Even then it has to be pretty specific for us to stick to it if we don't want to.

The crowd thins, leaving me to slide along the back wall toward the exit myself. The trek from here to the old team house isn't long, and I feel a need to stretch my wings, so I hoof it. I make note of the continued whispers of small groups finding their way back to work or home. Nothing in particular grabs my attention. I mull over everything that's happened today, including Zhen's predicament with Joseph.

I can feel the little pangs of regret and sorrow filtering through our bond. I savor each new emotion from my mate, knowing that his mind and heart are so open to me even after what I did. He amazes me every day.

There's such a gentle submissive soul inside that brick house of a man. My little scientist. I can't wait to show him everything. I know he's becoming impatient with me holding back on our bedroom adventures, but I refuse to push him too hard too fast. He's not fragile, but any new emotion other than pleasure or lust throws me when we're together. I find it hard to hurt him even when we both enjoy it because what if I'm wrong? What if I don't catch a more subtle feeling of displeasure or disgust and end up fucking it all up?

My phone vibrates in my pants pocket, pulling me from my thoughts. I have to wrestle the phone from my stretched pants, the material tight on my hips and thighs. I don't get as big as some of the others, but the change in pants size is enough to need stretchy material so I don't lose clothes every time I take my demon form. I smile at the sight of Zhen's picture on my screen, swiping to answer.

"Hello, my little scientist, how's it going?"

"I was actually calling because the bond felt weird, almost like you were worrying. Not scared, but . . ."

"Oh! You felt that, huh? Yeah. I was thinking about stuff and got to overthinking, I think."

"Stuff?" He doesn't call my ass out directly, but my mate is not a pushover. Submissive in no way means weak.

I chuckle. "About whether or not you're ready for more." I let my voice darken. "I'm torn between throwing myself headlong into my plans for you later and holding off for a little bit longer." His quick inhale and the thrum of anticipation that's not my own confirms his need for me to give him more.

"I'll take whatever you'll give me, *babochka*. I do eventually want everything, though. No more kid gloves?" His hesitant question makes me grin.

"I promise, mate. No more kid gloves. Now, you get back to what you were doing while I swing back to the Colorado coven house to check on things there. Stay with Belial and Rhys, please . . . Maybe don't spend *too* much time with the little Null, though. I don't think he'll be a good influence on you, to be honest. No filter, that one."

A squawk of protest sounds from the background, cluing me in to the eavesdroppers. I laugh loudly before hanging up, letting Z handle Rhys. He's the one who didn't tell me we weren't talking alone. I laugh again at the topic we were covering before my parting lines. I wonder when Rhys started listening.

Chapter Fifteen

Zhen

My cheeks are on fire as Az hangs up laughing. How
had I forgotten that Rhys was in the room this whole
time? I started talking to Az, putting him on speaker
like normal, and everything else faded away. I hadn't
even paid attention to the extra heartbeats in the
place.

"Oh hell, you should see your face. Priceless. Should I
take a picture? I should definitely take a picture.
You're so stinking cute. Don't be shy." Rhys cackles
like a loon while fumbling for his phone, ready to
carry out his threat.

"Oh, Rhys, leave him be. Don't embarrass the man. He
probably gets enough grief from Azvameth as it is.
Takes the patience of a saint to deal with that one. I
don't know how you do it, Zhenechka." Belial's soft
voice floats into the room before the demon himself
enters. His eyes dance with mirth.

Belial's soul is still breathtaking. He is filled with
gentle love, sharp stabs of jealousy and envy
constantly poking and flashing through it, but the
brilliant white stays firm. I can see the constant
struggle the envy demon endures and how it calms the
closer he is to Rhys. I cannot *see* his wayward envy
touch Rhys, only how his soul responds. Rhys's soul

almost seems to push something away kindly, not acting aggressive or mean . . . almost bored or like a habit. The way I've seen mothers herd children with ease and little thought. I smile at the interaction. The bond between the friends is peaceful and comforting. I could spend so much time just soaking up their easy demeanors and warmth.

Bel, still smiling, brings my attention back to his teasing. "So?"

"Huh?" So eloquent.

Rhys laughs. "He's asking if you have the patience of a saint. I can see it. You're steady, like a rock in a stream. That's good for Az because he's like a raging river most of the time. Never sitting still. I wonder. Does that restlessness and enthusiasm translate in the bedroom? He seems very . . . but you said kid gloves, so I assume you need dicked down harder? Let me tell you a secret—"

"Rhys! TMI, remember? He's not used to your questions or oversharing yet. It takes getting used to; you have to ease him into it. Don't scare him away, doofus." Belial almost sounds pleading. I assume he's been subjected to quite a lot of his friend's inappropriately detailed word vomit, so he has to be speaking from experience. I try to quell the blush I know I'm still sporting.

"What? No! He *needs* to know, Bel-Bel. What if he's not getting the good dick from his mate? How awful would that be? I'll help you, Zhen, don't you worry."

I feel forced to defend my sex life, which I really hadn't thought I'd ever have to do. "Oh! Umm. Thank you, but that's not necessary. I'm very happy with how Az and I are progressing. He's being very . . . patient with me." At Rhys's frown I know I didn't say it right, so I rush to continue. "He's doing what you said. He's 'dicking me down' just fine. Good. SO good. Awesome, even. I appreciate your wanting to help, I do, but I've got this. I, uh, I'll let you know if I need help with something."

A short nod is all I get, like something is settled. I have no idea what that means, and a shiver of apprehension runs through me. Oh, that's going to bite me in the ass later, but I need to distract him so we can move on.

"I do have a seemingly random question. Can I get a sample of your blood? Each of you? I'm working on a supplement to curb bloodlust. Astaroth is having me put it on the backburner, which is fine, but while we wait for the next soul here or an update on when we go to Reception, maybe I can gather some of the samples I need?"

"Of course! Here, where would you like me to put it?" I look over and catch sight of the blood suddenly dripping from Belial's wrist.

"Oh! I was planning on draw—it doesn't matter. A cup?" I stand quickly, searching for an appropriate receptacle. I can't keep the sample if it's gathered this way, but his willingness to help means I won't say a word.

"For crying out loud, Bel! You can't just drip everywhere. Go stand by the sink until it closes up. I think the doctor man needs to use medical equipment or something. All you're doing is *bleeding* all over a vampire. Get your shit together." Rhys has no qualms about calling the envy demon out, though, I guess.

I smile at Belial and pat his shoulder as it slumps. The wound has already closed up, so he just rinses the leftover blood off. My fangs tingle a bit and I feel a little hungry, but it's not too bad. "Thank you, Belial. He's not wrong, but I'm touched at the gesture." His sheepish smile is endearing.

I hear a heartbeat pick up from across the room. Then two. Three. The trio of wolves bursts into the room, led by Silas, his blue eyes flashing with violence. Beck and Joseph follow at a slower pace, though still quite quick.

"What the hell happened? Why were you bleeding?" Silas's cold tone sounds accusatory, definitely directed at me, but Belial flinches. Silas softens his tone, maybe. It seems warmer but only by a degree or two, I think. "Are you okay?"

Belial hasn't looked up, eyes still downcast at the sink. He gives a small nod, making him seem lost. A frown covers Silas's face . . . so it barely changed from his normal face.

"Leave them alone, Silas. No one did anything wrong. Take your grumpy ass right back out if you're going to be a frosty bitch." Rhys breaks the tension with his well-timed sass, making everyone laugh lightly. Not Silas, obviously. I think the last time the blond smiled was as a baby. Such a good soul housed in such a prickly little man.

"All right, bairns, settle yerselves down. I took the nap I was forced to take. You ready to go again, lad?"

I adore Joseph. I latch on to the redirection like the lifeline it is. I turn away from everyone else and focus on my friend. "Yes! Let's. Would you prefer to do so privately this time, or do you mind the audience?"

"If they want to watch, who am I to say nay? I don't mind, lad."

"All right, then let's get started. Sit or lie however you'll be comfortable for a while and I'll work around you, yes?" I don't know how this will go. Joseph will be whole again after this session if it goes as it should. I don't know what's going to happen once it's done.

After pulling a chair over to the sofa, I set my hand on his arm after he settles onto the cushions, arms crossed and breathing even. The voices of those around me fade away as I let my power do what it wants and I let my mind wander. A soul is a soul regardless of whether it's attached to a body. Since Joseph is still alive, I assume he will just continue to live his life but with less inner turmoil.

You cannot hear a soul until it starts detaching from a body, anyway, from my experience. While your soul resides in you, your body is the vessel. If your soul's tongue is cut, it won't be apparent in your mortal body . . . but once your body dies? It would need its own mouth and way of communication. My brain starts to hurt as I go round and round, trying to understand how a soul actually works. It makes sense, but there are things I'm missing. Energy?

I clear my mind as best I can and focus on Joseph. His soul is wiggling happily, excited and smooth. I watch as the gold color of my power does a final sweep before withdrawing back into me. Joseph's eyes pop open, glassy. A slow smile spreads across his face.

"Ye did it, lad. I know you did. I feel whole and healthy. Like I could run for miles and never tire. Thank you, thank you, thank you." He continues to murmur his thanks as he sits up, drawing me into a hug. I revel in the affection, squeezing him back. Elation runs through me in response to my own, and I know it's Az sending good vibes.

I let the sentimental moment continue as long as Joseph needs it, sinking into his fatherly love. As per usual, Rhys cannot contain himself. "Hey! I assume it worked?!"

I let my friend go, and we nod at the giant group staring at us. It seems like the whole house plus more of the demon team has gathered. Happy chaos ensues at our confirmation. Hollers and fist pumping from the demons, whooping from the residents of the safe house. Only Astaroth and Silas stand stoic. I would think they didn't care, except I catch the small twitch of the duke's lips and the desperate hope in the wolf's eyes.

Taylor runs and tackles Joseph in a hug, bouncing as he lands. Giggling and whispering, they share their joy. I watch with affection for a second before stepping back and searching for Az, feeling him enter. Our eyes lock, and the pride in his eyes warms me as he rushes forward in his demon form, picking up my stocky self and swinging me around. I laugh, letting him have his ridiculous fun. His tail whips around happily before wrapping around my waist. Only then does he set me down, loosening his arms while still making me feel trapped. My breath catches at the fire in his eyes.

"Let's go home, mate. I have a need to show you how wonderful you are." I nod frantically in response, forcing a laugh from him. "So eager, sweetheart." A portal opens behind me, and my mate starts shuffling us back toward it.

"Have fun, guys! Remember, no kid gloves!" Rhys's parting shout makes me groan in embarrassment once again, but I can't help the wave of heat at the reminder of Azvameth's promise.

I'm losing my mind. Azvameth is everywhere. Beautiful pain-pleasure races over me as his tail makes deeper cuts on my sides, his cock pounding at my hole at a devastating pace. He has two fingers in my mouth, rubbing my tongue in sync with his thrusts, pressing down harder with each inward stroke. Fangs slide up my neck, his hot breath tickling my ear, adding to the havoc that is my body. I feel like screaming as tears run down my cheeks when all motion stops. The orgasm that was right within reach fades away for the millionth time. A sob racks through me, my voice hoarse from begging.

"Shhh, sweetheart. One more time. One more time and I'll let you come. Look at you, crying so prettily for me." Az licks my tears and moans before starting the slow buildup again. Fingers leave my mouth to press into the cuts on my sides, playing with the blood that has dribbled everywhere. My mind is hazy, not quite tracking. A sharp pain on my length centers me again. I whimper and writhe, knowing I cannot go anywhere. My mate begins thrusting in earnest again, whispering filthy words as he brings his bloody fingers back to my mouth. I must have nicked him with a fang, because I taste the mix of our combined blood, drawing a guttural moan from me. I'm teetering on the edge, holding myself back because that's what he wants.

Right as I'm losing the battle against my impending orgasm, the sharp feather adorning his tail slaps straight across my slit. Pain explodes from my cock as pleasure courses through the rest of my body.

"That's right, sweetheart, give it to me. Coming so prettily for me" are the last words I hear or register as everything goes black, the pulsing in my ass signaling his orgasm. His low growl of completion comforts me as I drift away.

Azvameth

Legs shaking, I pull out of my mate's body as carefully and slowly as possible, watching the evidence of my orgasm leak out of him. Part of me wants to push it back in where it belongs, while another wants to lick him clean and then feed it to him. I won't, though I know he would love to be woken that way. I want him to rest, so I gently spread his thick cheeks with my hands. Using my tail to grab the wipes I keep next to every piece of furniture I could possibly fuck my little scientist up against, I clean up as best I can before placing the quickly emptying bottle of lube back in its home next to the wipes. I arrange our bodies so we lie comfortably away from the wet spot, turning into my human form to do so. Zhen is still on his front, head resting on my chest with his arm slung over me. His face twitches with each movement, no doubt feeling the aftereffects of "no kid gloves," while the bond hums in mutual satisfaction. I had been worried that the CBT and blood play were going to be too much, but I should have known my mate would be as into it as I was.

When I feel him start to wake through the bond, I know he's hungry for both food and blood. Excitement floods through me; I love feeding my mate. With his fangs so close to my neck, I just gently tilt his jaw to where I want him to bite and press his head toward me. He inhales deep, nuzzling my skin in thanks as he bites down. The pinch gives way to languid pleasure, and we both sigh. Keeping my hand cupping his neck, I feel each swallow, waiting for him to drink his fill. No longer dizzy from a single feed, I just enjoy the sweet bonding that a lazy feeding gives. Once done, he removes his fangs, licking my wound closed and kissing the spot with reverence. We bask for a little longer before his hunger for real food pushes me to get up.

"Rest a little longer, sweetheart. I'll get us something to eat." Feeding him human food has strengthened him as a mage considerably. Now that Zhen is no longer starving, his overall health shows in his skin tone and rosy cheeks. He still has most of the markers of a vampire but not the pasty sallow skin indicative of the species. I love watching him flourish under our love and attention. I'm under no illusions that the change in my mate is from me alone. I know his friendships play a huge part in healing the neglect he felt for twenty years. I still struggle to share him with others, but his happiness around them matters more.

Chapter Sixteen

Zhen

It's crazy what a difference a few days make. I've received the blood vials from each member of the team, plus a bunch from Astaroth's main office. Franco was an interesting person to talk to. He's so efficient and capable, so witty and nice . . . for a low-level demon. I have to wonder why he was sent to Hell instead of Neutral in the first place.

Between vigorous bouts of sex, I've been able to catch up on more reading from the books Azvameth gave me. The bond hums when I think of all our activities over the past few days. Even with accelerated healing, I'm still getting twinges hours later, which I honestly think contributes to the frequency in which Azvameth bends me over every available surface in the hotel and the farmhouse. If I think about any of it for too long, he'll pop up, grinning wickedly. His ability to suss out lust in our bond is top notch, and I'm not complaining. In fact I wish we could go over to the new place more often to do the same there, but Lily set the ward already and it won't include us until we get ready to do renovations.

Working with the souls at the safe house has actually been pretty productive. The total count of completely healed living souls is up to three. The two witches who always hid in the sunroom came to Rhys after

Joseph's healing and expressed their interest. Everyone else at the house decided to let them jump to the front because the women had families they could go back to once they were healed. Calls were coming in from the souls who had already gone back to their families; some were willing to come meet me and let me help them here at the safe house, while a few were understandably wary and wanted a neutral location. Rhys has been searching for a good second safe house, while Belial has been running back and forth between the alpha and beta teams' missions.

I try to keep myself focused on my own tasks instead of giving in to the curiosity plaguing me about what's going on with the demons who sided with Orobas and what information they got on Felicity. Tracking down and ridding the enemy of their witch would be an impressive leap in the right direction, though I know they've had a bunch of meetings about the missing alpha, too, so I don't know where that fits on the priorities list between the two demon teams.

Az is in charge of "extracting information" from less-than-cooperative captives, as has been his job for years. He doesn't seem to hate it even with his newfound emotions, and I'm actually grateful because it gives him an outlet, and I understand less-than-savory methods are sometimes the only option. If I don't think about it too hard, then I don't even feel guilty that he gets ramped up doing his work and I reap the rewards after.

"Daydreaming, sweetheart?" *Der'mo*. Of course. I roll my eyes and give an exasperated smile.

"*Babochka*. You know I'm allowed to feel turned on for more than a second without relief, right? You didn't have to come home just to love on me."

"Don't I? I cannot have my mate unsatisfied. It displeases me. I like knowing I've turned my little scientist into putty in my hands just because I can. Indulge me, will you?"

"You're ridiculous." I lean in to give him a quick peck, but he takes control immediately, fanning the flames until I'm nothing but an inferno. I give in, letting him take as he likes, and I feel his pleased hum against my lips. The pace slows until he is giving drugging kisses one by one, and I whine at the tease.

"Mm, delicious. I love tasting you, sweetheart." My dick throbs at the double meaning. "None of that now, you will have to wait." I scoff loudly because I know he's joking. He tweaks my nose and continues as if he didn't start all this. "I heard back from Franco a little bit ago. They have two departed souls you can meet at Reception. They've already started clearing the rooms. We can go now, or I can tell them to figure something else out. I want you to be able to help if that's your choice; I just don't want to push you into something you're not ready for."

I pat his cheek. "I want to go. Who are we meeting there?" I know it won't just be us, but I like to be prepared.

"Franco has vetted every single person on-site at Reception. Only the alpha team and Astaroth will be in the room while you do your thing. You'll probably have to talk with a few of the angels before you can see the souls, but I'll be right next to you the whole time."

Michael. I'm standing across the table from *the* Michael. Now I understand Lily's reaction to me, if this is what it felt like.

"Do you have any questions?" someone asks.

"Huh?" I'm an idiot.

Azvameth's chuckle is dark and dangerous, pulling my attention back to my mate. His brow is furrowed, and I feel violent jealousy streaking through him. Oh, shit. He thinks, well, I assume he thinks I'm awestruck over another man, and I am, but not for the reason he thinks. I push reassurance and love through our bond until his face relaxes.

"I, uh. That's *Michael*," I whisper, like that explains everything. I glance at the angel in question, and he gives me a soft, understanding smile.

"Oh God, this is too good. I took a picture in case you want to see your faces later." Rhys is cackling like a loon once again at my expense.

"Now, kitten. Be nice," Aridam chides, garnering a round of laughter from everyone present. His genuine confusion at our reaction makes Rhys laugh even harder.

"You're funny, big guy." He pats his large mate's chest before making grabby hands like a toddler asking to be picked up. An indulgent sigh escapes him as he gives in, but we all know he enjoys every bit of it. Once in his arms, Rhys gets back on track.

"Did you need any other accommodations? The room has a viewing window, but you need to pick the two people to go in with you besides Astaroth. I assume you want your mate, so pick another."

"Devland or Kek, please." I'd rather have Dev, but I don't want to insult Kek in the process. We have gotten over his initial visceral dislike of me, but I'm still not one hundred percent comfortable around him.

"If I must," Kek mutters. How enthusiastic. I roll my eyes internally.

Azvameth must feel it, because he steps in. "Yeah, Devland is my pick. No offense, Kek, but he needs to be able to relax completely and you might douche out again, so . . ."

"You can't just say it like that, Az. Have some tact."
Rhys clutches his imaginary pearls. Laughter again
from the group, lessening the tension.

Michael jumps in with a few suggestions but promises
everything will be fine. He's not alone, but I wasn't
introduced to the two angels with him. They are
probably important, but I'm trying to remind myself
that just because I'm curious doesn't mean it's my
business. "Mind ya business" is something I've heard
people say.

We settle into a conference room complete with table
and chairs and wait for Astaroth to bring in the souls.
The door clicks and smoothly opens, and I try to
smother my gasp. One soul looks like it was sent
through a paper shredder, while the other looks
meticulously taken apart manually. Eyes, ears, and
mouth missing. Limbs crushed and unusable. They
both stand shaking in front of me. I don't recall seeing
them when they were alive, but then again I don't
know if I'd recognize them whole and healthy. My
magic floods to the surface of my skin, itching to come
out. I stand quickly, startling them. They shrink back
against Astaroth, making my heart ache.

"I won't hurt you. I just want to help. Will you let me
help?" I don't know if they can hear me or feel energy,
so I round the table slowly, keeping my tone and step
light enough not to intimidate. They must feel the
vibration from the floor, because they turn their heads
toward me.

"Will you push the table and chairs to the wall, please?" I ask no one in particular. "I'd like to sit with them."

Astaroth gives a small nod, and the two demons begin moving furniture. The duke keeps his hand near where the souls stand. He can see them here in Reception but not touch them, so it must be out of habit. I reach slowly and touch the edge of the soul's arm like I've done a dozen times before now and will my magic to understand what I'm asking.

I sit as they do, letting my magic have full rein. The process is similar to before but more draining since I'm creating something from seemingly nothing. I sit for about ten minutes before I reach out and begin the process with the second, more shredded soul. I keep going until I feel my magic start to taper off, and a low, muffled grunt sounds from the soul with no mouth.

My head snaps up from where I'd let it hang, and I see how different they look. Their eyes remain unseeing, but you can see that they exist. Both of their arms have grown back to the wrist. Ears adorn their smudged head, pointed and small. Upturned nose and slim neck. They lean forward to hug me, and I realize the soul is female. I had no idea. The second soul looks more like I performed some rough patchwork, but there were definitely improvements made. Maybe more of the damage was internal? I'd be interested in getting their accounts so I can compare notes.

"Hell yes, Z! You did it!" I quirk a brow at Devland's very wrong but enthusiastic outburst. He just smiles at me and holds out a hand to help me up. Azvameth knocks his hand away with a quick growl and pulls me up himself, making Dev laugh.

"Hmm, 'it's' not done, but you did well, Zhenechka." Astaroth's voice conveys his pride. "Get together with Belial and Rhys to schedule in time for souls at Reception. We need more information as fast as possible. I have a feeling whatever they have planned won't wait long."

I nod emphatically and hold tight to Azvameth, knowing he'll whisk us away without a goodbye.

Azvameth

I'm soooooooooo bored. Like paint drying would be more entertaining. I know my mate thinks it's hilarious that I've been pushed off onto my regular beta team because the alpha team cannot handle my shit anymore. Apparently I whine constantly when not with Zhenechka, but if I stay next to him, I'm too distracted to actually protect him, and the others were getting annoyed by our sex breaks. Ridiculous. Who gets mad over sex breaks? So now I twiddle my thumbs at the Colorado coven house, just waiting for my own team to bring me people to torture.

The last one Kek dropped off is still unconscious, but hopefully he wakes soon or I will be going to check on Z, though I can feel he's fine through the bond. He must think my pain is funny. Fair, because I think his is sexy.

"He's awake," Shax murmurs. He's right. I missed him waking up, thinking about Z's delicious ass. Now that he's awake I'm annoyed that I have to push my mate from my mind. I know it doesn't make sense. It doesn't have to, Z said. Just has to make sense to us.

"Let's get started, shall we?" A giggle escapes me when I feel a thrum of arousal through the bond. Even my uptight mate likes when I . . . enjoy my hobbies. Such a good mate. I shall reward him later.

It only takes ten minutes before the witch breaks. Pathetic. I didn't even get to use any new tools. We did get the last known location of Felicity, though. Helel texted Bel the info the second the witch gave in, so I know they'll have someone check it out and soon. Probably Ari because he doesn't affect humans, but maybe they're caring less about getting caught. If that's the case, then Kieran can go. He can get any human to talk to him; it's just not subtle. Honestly I'm the better spy, but I don't have the patience for it.

Astaroth calls while I'm still contemplating going to Z, so I answer, hoping to be given a direction to focus this energy.

"Utah? What could possibly be in Utah?" Astaroth's disbelief rivals my own.

"Have no idea; that's just where he said. I didn't get the exact address, but Bel obviously didn't need it if he was able to track Felicity down this quickly."

"That was Lily. After we got the rough area, she was able to search for Felicity's magical signature. Quite a boon, having her as an ally."

I didn't even think of that. Good thing I'm not in charge. "So what's the plan?" I better be included.

"We have one, but I'm not sure you'll like it. Meeting at the new team house now that it's finished. Bring Zhen." He hangs up before I can question why. I shrug. It'll be a good place for him to hang out while I'm gone hunting, anyway. He's used to the safe house and our places, but the team house has better security than the others.

Leaving the mess for the beta team, I just portal to my mate. A round of gasps meets me, and I look around, confused. "You're covered in blood and still in demon form, *babochka*," my mate explains.

Ahh. Oh well. I take a step toward him but stop as he holds up his hand. I track his movements to the kitchen where he hands something off to Drystan. It must be the gluttony demon's day to watch Z and Rhys. I stay silent, still following my mate with just my eyes. His hand is still up, palm facing me. I want to bite it. He sidesteps to the door and places his hand on the handle, turning it slowly. I don't know what he's up to, but the bond is crazy with anticipation.

His muscles tense, and my prey drive kicks in. He's going to run. He told me about this fantasy a while ago, but I never thought he'd start it while people were around. He knows I will fuck him where I catch him. Vampire speed or not, I *will* catch him. Everyone else fades away as he flings open the door and vanishes. I burst after him, roaring his name. Adrenaline pumps through me, and I feel free.

I skid to a halt right inside the tree line and quiet down. Zhen could be anywhere in these woods, but if I don't trample around, I should be able to track him. I listen carefully. A rustling to my left is a small animal, so I ignore it. He never said I couldn't use my abilities to the fullest, so I leak out my power just enough to make me near invisible before I chuckle to myself and stop. He can hear my heartbeat and will be listening for it. There's really no stopping that. I listen again.

He's being incredibly quiet, which actually helps me find him. No animals at all to my right. No birds, squirrels, anything. The dead space tells me my mate is in a tree about one hundred yards northeast. I bend and pick up a rock, knowing the lack of heartbeat won't fool him but the sound should distract him for a second.

I chuck the rock toward the cluster of trees I'm certain he's in and take off running at the same time. Sure enough, a gasp sounds from the middle one as the rock hits a second before I get there. I scale the tree as fast as I can, watching my mate jump down and take off running again. I curse myself and follow, barely gaining on him. It takes longer than I thought to catch him, but as he leaps over a fallen log, I tackle him to the side. He grunts and tries to fight me off, only going boneless when I bite his neck hard as a warning. A shuddering whine escapes him, admitting defeat.

I waste no time collecting my prize, flipping him onto his front and ripping his pants away from his ass, not bothering to completely remove them. I check to see if he's loose enough to take dry and encounter a fully prepped hole. Ungh. "Such a good slut. Look at you, all prepped for me. I'm going to take you hard and fast like you need, okay, sweetheart?" Not actually a question, but he begs for it so sweetly just the same.

With no preamble, I shove my length into his greedy body. His ass sucks me in, pulsing already with the threat of orgasm. "You can come whenever you want, mate, but I will continue to use this hole until I'm done and not a second before, no matter how many times you explode." With that being my only warning, I set a brutal pace, reveling in the sweet moans coming from my little scientist. His back arched, throat exposed, ass tilted perfectly. He's stunning in his submission.

His first orgasm rips through him, and he shouts his release, body shaking. His arms no longer hold him up, so I follow him to the ground, using his beefy hips as leverage. I continue to slam into him, loving the way our skin smacks together. I know the hard ground has to be uncomfortable, but that just adds to my fervor. I want to see the scratches and bruises that nature will leave on him.

I feel the tingle start when his second orgasm courses through him, but I'm determined to see him through a third despite my earlier threat. I haven't touched his cock yet, so I force my hand under the waistband of his pants and squeeze, pinching his foreskin. He squeals and bucks, clenching impossibly tight around me. Not loosening my hold, I start jerking him. The friction must feel like sandpaper, but his moans and the amount of precum he's leaking show me how much he loves it. I continue to mutter possessive nonsense at him, knowing he languishes in my obsession with him. My wings begin flexing uncontrollably in my efforts to hold back, my tail thrashing. I pull my other hand from his hips and only use his cock for leverage, changing the angle of my upstroke. It must hurt just right because my mountain of a mate screams his third release and sobs, throwing me into my own orgasm.

I trace his cock during the aftershocks, gentling everything. I whisper kisses over his exposed skin, licking any blood from him. After pulling out, I lean down and clean him with my tongue, keeping my movements soft and sweet. His soft whimpers warm me, encouraging my worship of his giving body. I thank him in soft tones, putting him back together the best I can before pulling him into my arms. The dirt floor isn't the most comfortable, but I won't move until he's ready. He's awake but floaty, snuggling as close as possible and soaking up my continued praise.

After a bit I feel him come back to himself. I press a nibbling kiss to his bottom lip, waiting for him to open. When he does I pull his mouth to my chest, waiting for him to feed. He doesn't take much, but this part of our aftercare means a great deal to both of us, so I'm never willing to skip it.

I break the silence reluctantly. "How are you feeling, sweetheart?"

"*Da*. Good. Sleepy. So good."

I smile against his temple and settle in for a while longer.

Chapter Seventeen

Zhen

"It's not like he's a defenseless human, Az. He's a fucking vampire. Actually, he's a badass vampire who could probably kick a bunch of our asses just because he can *see your soul* so he can anticipate your next move, you stubborn fucker." Belial is adamant that I be included, and while I do appreciate it, I know coming from anyone but me, Az will balk.

"I can train with you guys today so you can see, *babochka*. I'll be fine." I push my need to help through the bond, and he grimaces.

"I hate this. I want it on record that I fucking hate this, understand?"

I kiss his cheek in thanks. "I know you do, mate. I do too. But it has to be done."

"Let's do it now so if you aren't coming, we don't have to plan the whole thing twice." I sigh at Kek, knowing he's going to actually be the one sparring with me. He trained with Rhys, so I assume he's the one we go to for this kind of thing. Great.

"Chin up, little scientist. Kick his ass." There's my supportive mate. I roll my eyes. The bond tells me he's struggling, but I know that. His face looks constipated, but he's slapped a smile on like I can't tell.

We all head toward the outdoor training facility they have on the property. Rhys and Ari did a really good job building the new team house. Spared no expense, of course, but the attention to detail is giving me some huge Franco and Belial vibes. The path winds down to a warehouse with soundproof walls and padding everywhere, including the ceiling. Fuck, sometimes I forget they can *fly*.

Kek stops and turns, waiting for me to do something. I just stare back blankly. He huffs and crosses his arms. "What are you waiting for, princess?" A low growl sounds behind me, but I know what he's doing. Baiting me into attacking first won't happen. I just arch my brow and adjust my eyes. His soul is unique, like every demon's. Pride is wrapped around his head, throat, and hands, almost strangling those areas. He must see the pity in my expression, because his face hardens and his arms drop, his soul flaring with anger. "They won't wait for you to be comfortable first. You won't have time to stare like an idiot. Attack first, give yourself the advantage."

"No. My job in all of this will not be to fight first. I'm not on the front lines. I'll only be engaging when necessary, correct? It only makes sense for me to go on the defensive. Attacking first will do neither me nor Rhys any good." I loop myself in with Rhys in case he has been trying to teach the Null to strike first. How silly.

Kek's face reddens before he transitions seamlessly into his demon form. His ebony skin turns a beautiful blue, his eyes glow a brighter violet, and his massive wings flex, showing off the intricate designs. I can still see his soul, so I make note that the pride wrapping around him slithers almost like a snake. His pants have stretched with him, and since none of these demons ever wear a shirt unless they're in public, he's ready.

In a blur he rushes me. I track him easily, used to seeing vampires use their speed in a fight. I don't move, waiting the mere second for him to reach me before we connect in a flurry of movement. I've always hated fighting without my elemental powers, but the past twenty years have conditioned me to be deadly without it. His soul telegraphs his movements a millisecond before he makes them, making it easy to anticipate his strikes and ducks. The fight seems to carry on longer than anyone anticipated because he pushes harder, adding more weight behind each hit. Sweat drips down my temples, but I don't tire. Being properly fed has bolstered my stamina considerably, not slowing me down.

I pinpoint the moment he stops thinking of this as a training exercise and goes for blood. He gives in to the pride snaked around him, and that shift is long enough for me to use my palm to push up and away as hard as I can. My intent had been to throw him far enough for me to have a second to reassess. Instead, when my hand touches his chest, it also touches his soul. We both freeze. I try to let go as gently as I can, not wanting to disturb the connection between his soul and his body.

We stare at each other, his violet eyes panicked and chest heaving. I try to convey my apology, patting his soul and sending in a small portion of my magic to fix any damage I may have caused. He shivers and gives a small nod. We silently agree to keep this to ourselves for now.

He turns to the group and glares. "So, he'll be coming with. Any other objections?"

They remain in shocked silence, and I wish Rhys would make a stupid joke to break the tension, but it ends up being Az. "Well, shit, little scientist. Do we have time for a quickie? I didn't know seeing you fight would make me so hot."

Everyone laughs. I get a few questioning and wary looks from team members I'm not closer to, but the knowing looks from Belial and Devland soothe my worry that the team will find out something happened and reject me.

Distantly, I hear the house phone ring, and Aridam portals to the house to answer while the rest of us slowly pair off and travel the short distance on foot. I need the fresh air. The bond quivers with Az's concern, but I push back reassurance and the feeling of *I'll tell you later*, which he thankfully accepts. We meander into the house and are greeted by Rhys and Wrath. Wrath, because his eyes look like liquid silver, holding Rhys in his arms like a toddler. Rhys looks excited, while Wrath looks bloodthirsty, for lack of a better word. His soul is itching for violence, only tempered by physically holding his mate.

"Shit, what happened?" Devland asks.

"They found her! Gear up, guys; I want everyone combat ready and back in here in five minutes. Belial and I will hold down the fort while you go get her and anyone with her. Hopefully this is a quick in and out, but we need to move before she does, capiche? You will be safe and stay in pairs, got it?!" Rhys's orders are met with fond smiles and slight nods. Only Az gives a smart-ass salute and mutters, "Aye, aye, Captain!"

I feel the bond flare with lust as I don my combat gear courtesy of Astaroth and Franco. The demons don't have much need for it, but I'll be a little more vulnerable. I know they've been working on obsidian-resistant gear for the guys, but sizing has been an issue, along with limiting their mobility. They won't wear the prototypes anyway, so it only takes seconds for most to be ready. Az helps strap the vest to my chest and takes care in covering my wrists and hands with flexible gauntlets. They're breathable and fingerless, which is nice. I flex my hands and marvel at the material. So cool.

Not willing to hold everyone up any longer, I rush back to where Az is holding a portal open, stepping through when he does. After a quick rundown of the plan they came up with in the five minutes I was changing, we set out.

I knew my part would be small; I'm just glad they're using me at all to confirm that we're grabbing the right witch and to scan for souls dark enough to be in league with her. It only takes a minute to approach the strip mall where she was seen using the shared office spaces for rent. Had she really stooped so low to have her end-of-the-world meetings at an actual strip mall in Utah?

We fan out, with Dev and me staying in the parking lot by the front entrance. He's in human form to help us blend in a little. They slapped S.W.A.T. on the back of my vest to help steer people out of the immediate area and to give a reason for a large bulletproof vest to be visible in broad daylight outside of a store. We're hoping it won't encourage people to come talk to us, but sometimes humans are weird as fuck.

Through the bond I feel like Az is excited enough he could be skipping. I hear the faint whistling of "Hi Ho, Hi Ho" from *Snow White* and know it's my mate making the noise, unable to contain himself. He's hopeful there will be bloodshed, but since we'll be taking at least one captive, he's claiming win-win since there will be blood later anyway.

I hear nothing more until Belial's voice sounds in my earpiece. "Target heading your way, Z. Keep an eye on the front." The door bursts open, and three people run out. Two women and a man. I immediately recognize

Felicity and one of her minion witches. The man's soul is dark but not evil. I rush with Devland toward the group. The man takes a defensive stance in front of the women. It seems they're not worried about magic exposure, because the other witch starts throwing spells with no regard to who could be filming.

Devland takes on the man, who I realize is a wolf, dispatching him swiftly. Unconscious but not dead. He forces Felicity to defend herself, leaving the spellcaster wide open. I use a burst of speed to slip past her spells, knowing any of them could probably kill me. My intent is to incapacitate her so she'll stop trying to hurt us, but as I grab her wrist and yank, my exposed fingers actually latch on to her soul, ripping it partly from her body. Not letting go like I did with Kek, I yank harder to see if I can actually sever the connection between soul and body. I feel resistance but I don't let go, even as Devland shouts in pain. I have to trust he can handle it or that Belial will send him backup. Felicity might be the face of this duo, but the witch I'm holding is stronger . . . much stronger.

With a final heave, her soul rips free from her body. Her body drops like the empty husk it is, and Michael appears a few feet away, assessing the situation. Surprise flickers over his face before he schools it. I refuse to let go of the witch's soul, afraid she will somehow be able to jump back into her body. No longer able to use magic, she is standing in shock, screaming.

Michael approaches slowly, holding out a hand to take the soul from me. I hold tighter, not wanting to give her up. The angel makes a soothing sound. "I've got her, Zhenechka. She'll go straight to Reception. I'll stay with her until Judgement, okay? I promise." I nod my assent and loosen my grip. The still-screaming soul and Michael are gone in a blink, forcing reality to rush back in.

Felicity is on her knees, two demons holding her down as she shouts threats and profanities. Az giggles beside her, rubbing his hands together like the murderous golden retriever he is. Kek is staring at the other witch's body lying close to me, standing with Drystan and Wrath. I overhear him explaining to the other two what happened while we were sparring. He comes closer and pushes the empty husk with his foot, showing them her face.

All three heads snap in my direction when I step toward them. "Michael has her. I, uh . . . Felicity was the leader, but whoever that witch was?" I point. "She was the power behind the combat spells, probably powering those illusions too. Her soul was strong enough. I, uh, I didn't know I could do that, you know?"

I feel drained and dizzy, but I'm not dead, so I'm not going to complain. My explanation is choppy and probably doesn't make much sense, but outside of the stares, I get a nod from Drystan and a smile from Wrath. Apparently all it took for Wrath to smile at me was to create a new kind of chaos. Who knew?

I'm lifted and swung around from behind, Az's deeper demon voice cooing in my ear. "You did so good, sweetheart. Not as bloody as I would have liked, but look how good you did!" His enthusiasm over my new homicide technique strikes me as funny, so I start laughing hysterically. I'm not happy I took a life, but I'm glad it was to protect someone I care about this time and not just because I was ordered to.

After Azvameth sets me down, his mouth immediately covers mine. His kiss is insistent and drugging; we don't pull apart until someone loudly clears their throat.

Kieran looks fondly annoyed. "I'd like to be able to get off this loud woman, please, if you could wait to fuck until a beta team shows up to grab her and the wolf man?"

Properly chastised, I go to pull away, but Az just grunts at his friend and glares until I wrap my arms back around his shoulders. "If I don't get to fuck you right here, then we're cuddling and I'm feeding you because you're hungry, understand?"

I can't help but laugh. "Thank you, *babochka*."

"Wrist or neck, sweetheart?" I debate for a second before just turning in his arms and holding up his wrist to my mouth. If I straddle him and feed from his neck, there's no way he won't bend me over immediately after, audience be damned. This way we don't upset anyone and Az won't have to fight his friends for seeing me orgasm even if it was his fault. I wait until we're settled on the ground before leaning back against his chest again and sinking my fangs into his wrist. Arousal thrums through the bond, but we keep it together, confirming I made the right choice. Az pushes me to take a little more than usual, claiming I overextended myself. I don't fight him on it, but I won't be drinking my fill. It would be too much at once.

"I'll take some iron and we'll do this again later, okay, sweetheart?" His sweet acceptance warms my heart every time he takes his vitamins. I've not touched bagged blood since he insisted he will be my sole blood provider. I don't blame him; I love the closeness it brings too.

The beta team shows up and gets ready to collect Felicity and the wolf. They wait by the portal, and I realize they are hovering for a reason. "*Babochka*, they're waiting for you." Surprise floats through the bond before a tentative questioning feel. I snicker because my demon mate is asking permission. "Go. I'll tell you where I'm headed after this once I know the plan." I get a mauling kiss in response before my mate skips away merrily.

"All right. Head back to the team house for a debriefing and some food, guys. We'll be waiting." Belial's voice sounds in my ear. I can hear Rhys shout that his mate better "hurry up or there will be no bajay" over the line at the end. Poor wrath demon almost trips over himself trying to go through a portal before it's fully formed. I don't know if a bajay is a boy vajay (I've heard from Rhys that that's a thing), or if it's just a weird way to say BJ. Either way, holding it hostage seems to make his mate panic.

Fascinating.

Chapter Eighteen

Azvameth

Shax and Helel lead me to the first open cell, throwing Felicity inside none too gently while two more beta members throw in the still-unconscious wolf. I let them lock up, and simply observe the witch now that her backup is gone. Watching someone while they realize they are totally fucked is always a pleasure.

Her face twists into a myriad of emotions, settling on a fake desperation. Ah, so this is how she is going to play it. I say nothing, just continue to watch. She is paying me little mind. I wonder if she knows who I am or if she's deemed me less of a threat with the other two here in their demon form. I slipped back into human form while she was losing her shit in the parking lot, so I'd be surprised if she knew what I was at all. So fun. Shax flicks a glance my way, and I subtly shake my head. I want them to take point on her questioning. Both demons are on a team that's working toward alpha status, so I want to see their dynamic. I'll step in if they need it, obviously. I'm not a monster. I snicker at my own joke.

Helel walks into the cell first, Shax following and locking it again after they are both fully inside. He tosses the keys to me through the bars. Smart.

"We want to ask you a few questions, Ms. Bianchi. I understand today didn't pan out like you'd hoped, but I'm here to offer you a deal for what you know." Helel speaks in a softer tone.

"Go fuck yourself, demon trash!" Felicity spits back.

"Oh, come now, Felicity. You know you're dying today, right? It's up to you how quickly that happens and with how much bloodshed." Shax's voice rolls out dangerously. Good cop, bad cop? Interesting approach.

"I won't say anything. You should just kill me now." The witch defiantly meets my gaze. Her eyes spark with recognition when I give her a wicked grin. She's right. She won't talk to them.

I chuckle darkly. "Perfect. I do so love a challenge. Envy, strap her up, please. Keep her hands immobile. Pride, would you be so kind to get the black bag at the end of the hall? I have a new toy I've been itching to try."

"But we—" Helel starts to argue, but Shax smacks his arm and points to the hall. Poor pride, he feels like he's not getting a chance to prove himself, but I'll explain later why it has to happen this way.

I unlock the door, keeping an eye on the witch as I trade places with Helel and hand him the keys. I wait for the snick of the lock to sound before I step toward our captive. I check her binds, adjusting where needed and explaining to Shax why we are tightening or loosening different places for the best results.

"Thank you, Felicity. I needed a guinea pig. I'm so happy you volunteered today. These two have never used one of my information kits. Did you know that? So sad. I was going to teach them on corpses, but it just doesn't give the same rush, you know?"

She pales as she sees the "bag" Helel is dragging into the cell. My kit has so many fun things in it. I can't wait to see how far I can push her before she breaks. I bend and slowly open the bag, letting the sound of the zipper be the only noise other than her heavy breathing.

"Let's start small. Pride, have you used a water pick? Fun twist: the water inside is actually hydrochloric acid. Oh! Or there's this!" I pull out a regular silver cuticle pusher that I've taken the time to file down to be razor sharp. I give a sweet smile. "For the manicure she needs. Which one would you like to do first?"

Helel looks a little uncomfortable, which is confusing. I'm offering to share my toys. He should be thankful. "No? You want Envy to go first?"

That gets him snatching the water pick. Pity, the cuticle pushers are more fun. "Good choice. Now, you only want to do one side. She needs to be able to hear our questions, you know?"

I let my power out fully, pushing it to the limit. I know it will make Felicity thrash around, agitated and unable to think straight. It will push her toward madness just like every other supe I've had to use it on as an interrogator over the years. Actually getting the pick into her ear will be harder, but she won't be able to block any pain. Furthermore her inability to stay still will only work in our favor since once the acid is in the ear canal it will slosh around.

"This, gentlemen, is why you need a sloth demon on your team."

Her screams start before he even turns the device on.
--
It took twelve minutes for her to break. Sobbing, she tells us everything she knows, slurring toward the end. Not as much as we were hoping, but we have a location for Gregory, the Albany alpha, and the confirmation that the angel's name starts with an A. Shax sets down the tiny blowtorch normally meant for desserts and wipes his brow. He's been quite the trooper, taking on the brunt of the work for the last seven minutes.

"She's tapped, Envy. Would you like to do the honors, or shall I?" Giving him first chance at killing her is so nice of me.

"Fuck yeah, I need her to stop screaming." He wastes no time, grabbing her head in his hands and snapping her neck. He straightens and shakes his head like the sudden silence is weird.

"Good job, both of you. I'll clean up the weapons and call another beta team to clear the cell. Take the rest of the night off, maybe go get laid." I waggle my eyebrows, pulling weary laughs from them.

Cleanup doesn't take long. I throw everything into the dishwasher, which is its sole purpose now. I wouldn't eat off anything it's cleaned, but it sure does do the job quick. The two beta teams that responded to my summons lounge in the living room, waiting for me to direct them.

"I need two to clear out the cell and burn the crazy lady's body while another two keep an eye on mister wolf. I'll be back for him tomorrow. If he says anything or wakes before I return, let Franco know and he'll send me a message." At their nods, I portal to the team house, trusting they'll get the job done.

My mate is curled up on the couch, taking up the whole thing. He must feel me near, because his eyes flutter open and he gives me a soft smile.

"Want me to help you shower, *babochka*?" His voice is thick with sleep.

"I'd love your company, but if you need to rest . . ." I smirk as he attempts to scramble off the couch. The cushions are deep enough that they've sucked him in, so I lend a hand, wrapping him in my arms once we're standing. I kiss his temple, sliding my hand down his arm to tangle our fingers before pulling him toward the portal I've opened to the hotel room.

We walk straight into the bathroom, stripping silently as we take each other in. It's been a long day for my little scientist, and I want to pamper him a bit. He discovered a new thing he can do with his soul powers, and while I know it scares him a bit, I'm so in awe of him. He hasn't stopped amazing me since I pulled my head out of my ass not that long ago. Every single day, I still regret rejecting him.

"None of that, now. We're exactly where we are supposed to be, love. Listen to the bond. It's healthy and happy, strong," Z soothes me, kissing my shoulder lightly.

"I love you," I whisper softly, finally saying it out loud.

"I know. I love you too, *babochka*."

I hum in response, enjoying how his hands are now running up my neck to tangle in my hair. Massaging my scalp, he turns me into a puddle of floaty horniness. Such an odd combination, but he revels in it. Ninety-nine percent of the time, I'm the one taking charge, but occasionally my little scientist insists on taking care of me. We always make slow, sweet love, him undulating on top of me, letting me bask in the feel of his big, tight body. I whimper in anticipation. I need that slow love right about now, and he knows it. His smile is soft but smug as he finishes washing and drying me, leading me slowly to the bed.

Zhen

My sloth demon is rarely so compliant. So soft and relaxed, he lets me maneuver him onto the bed, legs splayed open for me to enjoy. His eyes lazily track my movements as I grab the lube from the bedside table.

"You going to open yourself up for me, sweetheart? I want to see."

I had planned on prepping myself quickly, but I alter the plan to give him what he wants. Turning to straddle his thighs, facing his feet, I lean forward to bare myself to him. Rough hands skim over my thighs, encouraging me. Making sure to get enough slick covering my fingers, I prep my hole as slow as I can manage. I only get to two fingers before I'm shaking with the effort of holding back, whimpering because I just want to impale myself on him. I want the stretch, the burn of entry to center me before he fills me up.

"You're doing so well, sweetheart. So good. Look at you." His hands are still running up and down the backs of my thighs, occasionally wandering around my ass and lower back. His touch soothes and sets my blood on fire. Trying to add a third finger at this angle is hard, even with my chest pressed into his shins.

"Come here, mate."

Finally. I almost sob in relief as he pulls me by the hips closer to his chest. My body relaxes, and I let my hand fall away as he takes over. He spreads my cheeks wide, petting my hole with his thumb.

"So soft, so sweet," he murmurs to himself.

I concentrate on the sensations he's giving me, whining when he pulls away. Cold lube hits my hole before he gently inserts three of his fingers into me, tugging on the rim. He grows, the body beneath me getting larger, and the cock that was trapped under my chest pulls free, slapping near my face. I tilt my head up to capture just the tip, suckling sweetly while he groans. He never quickens his pace, but his pulsing cock betrays his impatience.

After he deems me ready, he slides up to rest against the headboard, pulling me down onto his lap in the process. Even with all that prep, his demon cock burns in the best way as he enters me. He gives me a chance to lean into the pain as he pulls my legs to the outside of his, my back to his chest. Soft kisses adorn my neck, his breath hot on my ear, eliciting a full-body shiver and a low moan from me. I must clench against him, because he answers my groan with one of his own.

"Slow, sweetheart. I want to feel you." My hips move without thought, following his direction. The drag of his shaft against my prostate with every thrust pulls the craziest noises from me. So good. I could stay just like this forever. I feel my orgasm right out of reach, drifting closer and closer.

Az's tail runs softly up my inner thigh, adding a unique sensation to our coupling. I never know if his tail will lash out with painful pleasure or if it will continue its languid caress, and I love the element of surprise. I can see the tips of his wings flex with pleasure as they block my peripherals. I soak in the feel of his horns against my temple as he leans down to suck the mating scar on my neck. My orgasm rushes through me, wave after wave breaking against my skin. I'm drowning in the pleasure, feeling Az pick up his pace for a few thrusts, using my body to achieve his own release.

He continues to fuck lazily into me, prolonging our orgasms as long as possible, milking me dry with the help of his hand on my cock. His right wrist presses against my mouth while his left arm bands tightly around my torso. "Drink, sweetheart. I'll stay inside you the whole time."

I sink my fangs into his skin, loving the flex of his shaft inside of me as he reacts to my bite. He continues to shower me with praise and gentle touches as I drink. I sink further into his embrace, luxuriating in this moment.

Refusing to leave my body, my mate arranges us in the bed without dislodging his cock. "Rest, my little scientist. I'll wake you when it's time to get ready to go." I let his warmth lull me to sleep.

Chapter Nineteen

Azvameth

"What information did the wolf captive have for us, Azvameth?" Astaroth starts the meeting with no preamble.

"Not much, actually. We had already gotten Gregory's rough location from Felicity. The only piece of new information is a mere rumor. He apparently overheard a few conversations the witches were having while he was guarding them. He claims they have been working on exposing the angel, but other than his name starting with an 'A,' they have no idea who he is. He never met with anyone outside of Constantine as far as anyone knows. Even Zhen said he only saw him with Constantine. We do have conflicting descriptions . . . though I'm more apt to believe Zhen's account than anyone else's.

There are also rumors that journals filled with information from Constantine are somewhere in one of his estates. I highly doubt he just squirreled away a spiral notebook full of important shit, but I sent a beta team to look for them anyway, just in case. It will take some time." I'm disappointed with the lack of intel I have for our duke.

"Very good. How is Zhenechka progressing with the souls at the safe house? I see he has already healed another soul from Reception completely."

I smile. "Good. He's hoping either Beckett or Silas will be next, but they keep allowing others to go first. We may want to get a shrink in there to see if they're being martyrs or just stupidly polite." I can't see Silas being a martyr, but how should I know? He doesn't strike me as the polite type either. Maybe there's more to him than being a frigid little shit. Doubt it, though. Some people are just dicks.

Astaroth's laugh shows I didn't offend him. "I'll let Rhys know. I'll be sure to use more tact, but I'll impart your wisdom."

"He actually already has it on the books for next week. Rhys did notice that our two remaining wolves seem to be putting off their healing sessions. He believes they may just be scared, but Taylor has also been pulling himself back, so we want to make sure there isn't an underlying issue." A frown mars Belial's face on the screen. With Rhys unable to join us here in Hell and Bel not liking attending meetings without his Null buffer, this video chat is our compromise. I have no idea how the technology works, but I don't care enough to look into it.

A text notification sounds in the room. I have everyone silenced except for my mate, so I know it's him. I pick up my phone from where it lies on Astaroth's desk.

Little Scientist: *Quick question. Rhys asked and I don't know the answer. Do we have a timeline for finishing the farmhouse? I haven't even thought about it, but I haven't heard from Dane in weeks. Have you?*

Me: *No, that's really weird. Franco was going to call when Dane was done, but that should have been while we've been at the hotel. I'll ask Franco when I get done here with Astaroth.*

Little Scientist: *Thank you. I'm worried since no one I've talked to has seen him. Let me know as soon as you find out. Please.*

"Hey, Astaroth, I need to ask Franco a question. It might be urgent. Will you page him?" Wait. I turn to the screen. "Actually, you might know something, too, Belial. Have you heard from or seen Dane lately? Zhen is worried since he was supposed to start working on the farmhouse quite some time ago, but the wards Lily set haven't notified us of someone even coming close to the property line."

Belial freezes and his eyes widen. "Fuck! No. Shit. Okay, uhh, he was supposed to be here recently . . . let me check real quick . . . over a week ago to visit with Beck, and he never showed. With everything going on, we must have missed him. I assumed Rhys called him and thought Dane was just waiting until things calmed down to visit again. I'll start trying to track him down right now. Fuck. I'm signing off. Let me know if Franco—just let me know." The screen goes dark.

Astaroth is already up and shouting out of his office door toward Franco's desk. "Find him! We cannot allow anyone to slip through the cracks. I want every single rescued soul talked to and accounted for *today*. Today, Franco!" The duke whirls around and slams the door, hands shaking.

"We need more hands on this. I'm pulling in two more beta teams and an alpha team. We will find them or so help me—" He cuts himself off, sitting in his large chair and pulling out his phone. I can tell I've been dismissed, so I portal back to Zhen at the safe house. I know he won't take this well, but he's already doing everything he can to help these people.

He must feel me close, because he and Devland rush into the room, followed closely by Beckett and Silas.

"He's missing, isn't he? I had a terrible feeling; I wish I would have said something sooner." Beckett's voice is thick with tears. Dev rushes to reassure him, opening his arms for a hug. Beckett falls into the greed demon's arms, losing his battle with his tears as they overtake him.

"So what's the plan? Are there more?" Is that concern on Silas's face? No way.

"We are bringing more people in. Franco is personally calling every rescued soul today to get a headcount.

217

We are hoping it's just Dane missing, but honestly there has been so much going on, we might have missed more." Shame flows through the bond, and I snap my head up in time to watch Z's face crumple. I grab him and pull him to me, kissing his temple.

"It's not your fault, little scientist. We'll find him and anyone else we might have missed. We won't let them stay lost, okay?" My tone is firm, begging him to believe me. I hate feeling his distress. I want to murder something. Anything. A severed head is better than flowers, right? Right. That. We'll do that.

A watery chuckle leaves Zhen's lips, making me look at him questioningly. "I can feel you flip-flopping between murder, excitement, and panic. What are you thinking?"

"That I would do just about anything to make you stop feeling responsible. My mind just went off track trying to connect romance and torture," I admit sheepishly.

He must think my ideas are brilliant, because he gives me a sweet smile before patting my chest. "I'll be okay, *babochka*. Like you said, we'll find him. I believe if anyone can, it's you guys."

"Is there anything we can do here to help?" Beck offers softly. His eyes are puffy and pink, splotches covering his face. He's really not a cute crier. Was he particularly close to Dane, or is he just emotional? Needing to see if it is indeed just him, I glance at Silas and am met with an icy blue stare, cold and unfeeling.

I physically cringe but refuse to break eye contact. Zhen notices and follows my gaze, surveying the stare off between me and the little asshole of a wolf.

He giggles. "Az, leave him alone." I grunt in response, trying not to blink and failing miserably.

"He's so fucking *mean*, Zhenechka. Look at the little fucker." I glare harder at the defiant blond. His mouth twitches, and it's enough to make me believe he would have smirked if he had less control of his face. He starts to look mildly disgusted, and I didn't even *do* anything.

"Fuck you!" I want to fight him. I don't know why he pushes every button I have, but I want to fucking fight him.

The little shit just blinks at me blankly, like I'm overreacting. My skin itches with the need to smack him around. That'll show him! He tilts his head slightly, taking a step forward. I step back, then growl at my show of weakness and take two steps toward him. He looks up because he's short as shit and whispers, "Go ahead, sloth. I'd love to play patty cake with your intestines." His whisper is barely there, and he didn't move his mouth. I'm, like, one hundred percent certain no one else heard him. He's using my advanced hearing against me. He opens his arms like he's offering a hug, and I feel trapped between how crazy I'll look if I kill him now and how satisfying it would be.

Zhen sighs happily, patting Silas on the shoulder before looking at me. "Don't be mean, Az. You'll love him once you get to know him. You'll see."

The fuck I will! I shove Silas's arm away, refusing the clearly fake offer of friendship. Sneaky little shit.

Everyone still gathered makes disappointed sounds and sighs, riling me up more.

Zhen

I couldn't hear what Silas said to Az, but I've been watching his soul. He's having so much fun tormenting my mate that I have to go along with it. They're a lot alike, actually, and I think they really will be good friends eventually . . . if they don't kill each other first.

I sigh like I'm disappointed when Az refuses to hug Silas, making him scowl harder. I try to hold back my amusement at their antics so that he doesn't sense it through the bond. My mate's agitation is only going to benefit me later, so I have no incentive to soothe him right now. Besides, Silas really is a good guy, and Az needs someone to poke at him. Keep him on his toes.

"If there's nothing else we can do today, we may as well just meet back here tomorrow. We can go from there. If anything happens between now and then, let me or Azvameth know and we'll be right over. Are you guys going to be okay on your own?" I address mostly Beck since Silas doesn't talk around Az that much, likely just to piss him off.

Devland cuts in. "I'll stay here with them tonight. I'd feel better if we had someone on the team who can open portals here who isn't . . . well . . . coupled up. We'll have a movie night or something." Beck's shoulders slump in relief at hearing that the greed demon is staying. Even the lines around Silas's eyes lessen.

"Perfect. Then we're leaving." That's all Az says before grabbing me and throwing me over his shoulder, marching straight to the portal he opened next to us. I wave as we leave, knowing they don't really take offense that we rarely say goodbye properly.

Instead of one of our places, the portal opens to a random park. It's hot and muggy, leading me to believe we are close to the equator. Az sets me down on my feet and lets me find my legs before he answers my unspoken question.

"I, uh, have wanted to bring you here for a while, but the timing has always been off. It's still off, but . . . it's just, we already said we can't do anything until tomorrow. Anyway, we're here now, so I want to enjoy it with you." He sweeps his hand to the side like he's showing a display piece at an art show. "We're at Tradewinds Park. It's actually one of my favorite places in the world."

Catching on, I gasp and turn to see a large white sign with teal letters scrawling out Butterfly World. The monarchs on the sign leave little room for guessing. Butterflies. My mate brought me to see his butterflies.

I can't make my voice work, so I flood the bond with everything I'm feeling. He smiles softly at me and wraps me into a hug before settling me under one of his arms. It's a tad awkward with our matching heights, so I tangle our fingers together instead. He swings our arms gently as we walk in. Taking our time, he leads me around to every exhibit they have to offer, going slow and pointing to each species he can identify. After I think we've seen everything, he leads me to a gate clearly marked Staff Only. Plenty of people are milling about, so I'm confused as to why no one seems to notice or care.

"No one will bother us. I'm pushing out a bit of power to give us some privacy. This is the last place on the kind of tour. All the butterflies come to this area to rest and eat when there aren't a ton of visitors. The humans don't know why." He winks and points. "I keep that log right there well stocked with flower nectar so they continue to flock here." We make our way over to the log and sit gingerly, trying not to spook anything.

"It's beautiful, *moya lyubov*. Thank you for bringing me here."

"*Moya lyubov*. That's 'my love,' right?" I nod and he smiles. "I like it. Almost as much as *babochka*." He gives me a sweet kiss before getting distracted. "Oh, look, zebras! They're so cool, Zhen. They can live like ten months, not just the standard seven to fourteen days of some of the more common butterflies."

I marvel at how peaceful the bond has grown since we've been here. Normally I can feel him jittering or restless in the background, but here he's almost serene even when chattering about the different life spans and diets of rare butterflies.

I sit next to my mate, leaning into his side, and soak up this perfect moment.

Epilogue

Zhen

"You're almost ready, aren't you, Cynthia?" Az coos into the butterfly tent set up in my lab. I want to regret surprising him with a butterfly area because it takes up so much time and attention, but he loves it so much that I can't. It also gives me time to work on my own research while still spending time with my mate.

His chair creaks as he bends down further to check every chrysalis in the tent. He's named them all, which is adorable. We have a few days left before they emerge as butterflies, but that doesn't stop him from having full-blown conversations with them each day. He has even given them a play-by-play on what happened with Orobas's sentencing. He showed them the video of him being transformed into a shadowling. I didn't even know you could record something like that. He got the video from Franco, I think, so it must have been fine. Probably definitely not breaking any rules.

"How long do you think they have left, *babochka*? Do you think they'll hold out until we get back on Tuesday?"

"Why would I need to wait? I'll come back and check on them each day." He's genuinely confused.

"You already have nanny cams up and connected to your phone. I thought you would just check in on them that way?" His scandalized look shows I'm an idiot. Of course, if he can portal back at a moment's notice, why not? It's not like the *twelve* cameras are enough. I thought he was kidding when he said he got one for each chrysalis. Silly me.

"Those are for all the time! What if they miss me or get lonely? Hmm? What then, mate?" The thing is, I still don't know if he's joking.

"Ahh, my mistake. How right you are." It's better to just give in. He's been saying goodbye to them for entirely too long. We're already late.

"Why are you just standing there, little scientist? Time's a wastin'!" His shit-eating grin is wide on his face.

"I'm not—gah! You're the one taking forever. I've been ready for ages!"

"Come now, let's not point fingers. That's not very nice, sweetheart." His voice lowers and takes on a sultry quality, immediately derailing my blood from anywhere else in my body directly to my cock. Mind blank, I just stare at him, trying not to drool. There is something we are supposed to be doing, but I can't for the life of me remember what it is.

My mate stretches his hands above his head, letting me watch his muscles ripple with the action before

225

holding his hand out, palm up. "Come, sweetheart, we have to go. We can play later." I whimper but take his hand, ready to follow wherever he's leading me.

I'm able to dial down the lust from a nine to a three by the time we walk up the porch steps of the safe house. We are making a few stops today before we head out to stay at Reception for a few days. We only have six more souls there and are trying to focus on them while we wait for news on Dane. Everyone else was accounted for, which is good, but it makes the one person missing that much harder to find. Our team and the old Albany pack are working together to find him; they're working as hard as they can, but he's been missing for two weeks and a few of our guys are losing hope.

"Rhys! Do you want to see the pictures I took this morning?" My mate runs ahead, spotting the Null in the dining room.

"Umm. Sure! Yes, I would love to look at the same thing a million fucking times." His sarcasm is lost on Az. He just nods like that's perfectly reasonable and pulls his phone out to show him. I wisely change directions, looking for Dev and the wolves who always seem to be with him. I don't want to be sucked into butterfly watch either. I hear Silas snicker from the living room, so I head that way.

"No one wants to see your asinine pets, sloth. Wait until they hatch; then they might be a little bit interesting . . . but I doubt it." Silas's face is so gleeful as he dryly insults my mate. I try not to laugh as a crash sounds from the other room. The wolf jumps up and takes off running out the sliding doors, not bothering to close them. Wise choice, as my sloth demon comes barreling into the room on a rampage.

"I'll fuck you up, you little shit!" he roars.

"You have to catch me first, old man!" Silas's voice drifts on the wind.

I giggle, knowing by now that Az won't actually hurt him . . . if he can find him, anyway. Silas is incredibly talented at evading my mate, much to his dismay. I settle in to talk to Dev and Beck while I wait for Az to return, noting how close the two men are on the couch. I wonder if there's something there. I'll have to keep an eye on them. I don't want either of them to get hurt . . . but they're grown-ass men, so I'll stay out of it. Hell help them if Az picks up on it, though. They'd never know a moment's rest.

We visit a while before Silas returns without Az. He's sweaty and disheveled but looks to have no injuries. Good for him. He quickly heads upstairs, out of sight, before my mate stomps in . . . *completely* covered in mud.

"What the hell, Azvameth?! Go hose off or something outside!" Rhys shoos him out of the house. I can't hold it back any longer and burst out laughing. My side hurts by the time I calm down enough to follow my pouting mate outside.

"Let me help, *babochka*. I've got you."

AUTHOR'S NOTE

Thank you everyone for coming back to read *His Sloth*! I hope you enjoyed it; please leave a rating and review so others can too!

It took a bit longer for me to understand the dynamics between Az and Zhen. There was a lot more struggle inside the relationship instead of external problems which was crazy to see unfold. Honestly, they almost didn't make it but I'm *so* glad they did.

WANT MORE?!

This is part of an 8-book series following our favorite team of demons.

Next up?

We see what Devland will do when his heart is screaming for him to claim a man that isn't his mate in *His Greed*.

Xoxo,

Ava

RUSSIAN TRANSLATIONS

Babochka - butterfly

Bezhat – run/escape

Da - yes

Der'mo - shit

Izvinite - I'm sorry/ my apologies.

Moya Lyubov - my love

Nyet - no

Plez - please

Pomogite - help us